TALES
LIES

S.S. DAVID

ArrowGate

Published by Arrow Gate Publishing Ltd

London

Copyright © **S.S. David** 2023

13 12 11 10 9 8 7 6 5 4

First published by S.S. David, 2012
Second Edition by Arrow Gate Publishing Ltd.

S.S. David has asserted her rights under the Copyrights, Designs and
Patent Act 1998 to be identified as the author of this work.

Arrow Gate Publishing's titles may be repurchased in bulk for educa-
tional, business, fundraising, or sales promotional use. For information,
please email info@arrowgatepublishing.com

British Library Cataloguing-in-Publication Data
A CIP Catalogue record for this book is available on request from the
British Library

ISBN 978-1-913142-30-8
eBook 978-1-913142-31-5

www.arrowgatepublishing.com

Arrow Gate Publishing Ltd Reg. No. 8376606

Arrow Gate Publishing 85, Great Portland Street, London W1W 7LT

To Kayroy, with all my love

What you leave behind is not what is engraved in stone monuments but what is woven into the lives of others.

—PERICLES, GREEK STATESMAN 495 BC

TALES OF
FIVE
LIES

S.S. David's first novel, *The Impossible President,* a best-seller, ran out of print-run within a week. The second edition is coming soon. She has written other works of fiction. *The Feet of Darkness*, and *Cydonia: Rise of the Fallen*. David is writing another full-length novel and a collection of short stories. She lives in London with her husband and three children.

www.seyisandradavid.org

https://www.instagram.com/ssdavidreads/

https://twitter.com/seyi_sandra

https://www.facebook.com/seyisandra.david

PART ONE

THE SIGHTING

I shouldn't have agreed to my friend's ludicrous idea.

The evening sky had turned a dark, foreboding shade of grey as I stood by the window, staring at the skyline of Huntsville, Alabama, that cold October night. It was barely visible, shrouded in a thick fog that seemed to swallow everything in its path. The wind was picking up speed, howling like hordes of hell on marching practice before an invasion, causing the trees to sway and creak in the eerie darkness. I shuddered more from fright than the cold weather.

My overactive imagination saw a pack of wolves advancing towards my house, sending chills down my spine. I closed my eyes and reopened them. Thankfully, there was nothing: the night light was playing tricks on me. I shook with fear as I thought about why I said yes to Lola's foolish suggestion of exploring the nearby woods at midnight.

I turned away from the window. The gloomy weather matched my mood, and I felt uneasy about what my friend

Lola had asked of me. She'd arrived at my doorstep earlier that day in a dishevelled state with torn black jeans, a dirty trench coat, and a chaotic high puff hairstyle. A strand of hair hung near her right eye, which she impatiently tucked behind her ears. Her dark skin seemed to glow in the dim light, but her eyes were red, puffy, and bloodshot. Without telling me what I was about to do, she begged me to go into the woods that night, causing my anxiety to grow.

I had a feeling something was wrong. Lola loved the latest fashion, and her impeccable taste was the envy of everyone who knew her. If I hadn't known her for thirty years, I would've bet she was on crack cocaine or other dangerous drugs. Alarm bells started ringing in my ears. I touched both ears briefly and hoped my tinnitus wasn't back.

Lola must be throwing someone off her scent and merging with the crowds. I thought, but discarded the idea. I lived in the leafy, secluded part of Huntsville called Greywood Drive. A gated community with affluent, entitled, wealthy, snobby, elite members of the city. Lola's house was a five-minute drive from mine, and she was popular. Everyone knew and coveted her presence at their parties and charity events. A friend once described Lola as *oxygen*. I couldn't agree more. She attended the best parties and loved to sing, and as the best criminal lawyer in Huntsville, everyone wanted to be her best friend.

Whatever prompted her to camouflage as a homeless person must be serious. I checked the window and saw her Range Rover and smiled. *How can a homeless person be driving the latest Range?* The situation was absurd. I felt disappointed that Lola didn't come up with a clever disguise to fool her 'pursuers'.

"You could have called," I said when she came in, looking like a low-paid, weather-beaten detective on the tail of a serial killer. Sniffing around, she appeared to be looking for clues that weren't there. Lola's reaction was similar to a scene from an apocalyptic film. I grimaced, groaned, coughed, and cleared my throat. I was at a loss for what to make of the unfolding scene before me.

"You'll thank me later, Christine, for the trouble I've gone through to warn you," she said. Her attitude exuded an air of mystery. I waved her to a sofa, but she declined and went to the kitchen. I'd made French macaroni cheese, and it smelled divine. I hoped it would tempt Lola to take a quick bite. But I sensed food was the furthest thing from her mind.

"Your Range Rover would easily give you away," I said. Then I noticed the black gothic chunky boots. "Why didn't you call an Uber?"

The only thing left for Lola was the classic American bike with chains to complete the look. I felt a strange sensation crawling up my spine. *What on earth is going on?* I thought with a shudder but clamped down on my emotions and wore my blankest expression. I'm like an open book, and Lola can read me easily.

"No, an Uber will take a long time," she answered. I heard her rummaging through the kitchen cabinets. Her behaviour was showing signs of agitation and restlessness. I followed and saw her with my large, six-inch knife, which I used to carve Thanksgiving Turkey.

"What's happening?" I asked with a tone of alarm in my voice. I moved toward her and took the knife from her trembling hands. "What's going on, Lola?"

We stared at each other for a long time. Without a word, she walked away from me. She went to the living room and sat on the sofa, her eyes fixed on the Windsor Grandmother clock my dad gave me on my wedding day; well, not my dad, but his good friend, Professor Bradley, presented the clock to me. I clenched my jaw and gritted my teeth. I must unravel the mystery of the century.

"What is it? Why all this?" I asked. Waving my hands at her appearance.

Lola rocks back and forth when faced with indecision. I saw her battling with the urge to divulge every detail. She closed her eyes, and when she opened them, I noticed the taunt jaws, clenched fists, and constant rocking.

"You have to go to the woodlands at midnight. Make sure no one knows. Your life depends on it," Lola whispered. Her lips barely moved. There was a glint in her eyes, and I recognised that. It was the look of determination, *the fight-to-the-end* kind of look. She always had that before a major case. Suppose she was trying to pique my already over-inflated ego, and boy, did I buy into that? I did without a doubt.

Lola's unusual request for me to go to the woodlands behind my villa at midnight had aroused my curiosity. She insisted that it was a matter of great urgency. When I suggested telling my husband, Ashley, she became agitated and pleaded with me to keep it a secret. I agreed, not wanting to upset her any further.

She left with a promise to call me in the morning. I watched her walk to her car, and Lola gunned the Range out of my driveway. I tried to make sense of the motive behind Lola's story. Nothing added up. Venturing into the woodlands at midnight, making sure no one sees me. The clandestine warlike operation doesn't sound like me, but I must see this through. There was no other option available to me. I had no choice.

After dinner, I settled on the sofa with my nine-year-old son, Shiloh. We curled up together, with him nestled close to my side, his small frame pressed into mine. The room filled with the familiar theme tune of his favourite cartoon, Mickey Mouse, and we both relaxed while watching the cheerful characters on the screen.

When the episode ended, I scooped him into my arms and carried him to his room, his head resting on my shoulder. His room was cosy, with pastel walls and shelves adorned with his favourite toys and books. I laid him down on his bed and reached for his well-worn copy of 'Gruffalo', a story we'd read countless times before.

I sat down beside him and pulled him close. His warm little body snuggled up to mine. As I opened the book, I could feel the apprehension building inside me. I pushed away the terrible thoughts and fears that plagued my mind, focusing instead on the familiar story we both loved.

I began reading, taking my time, emphasising the different characters and their personalities. Shiloh fixed his eyes on the pages, his expression intense, as if he was living the story with every word. When I finished, he looked up at me with those expressive eyes, and I realised that he, too, felt the weight of the moment.

"I love you, Mum," he said. His arms reached for a hug. I wrapped my arms around him tightly, feeling the warmth of his body and the beat of his heart against mine.

"I love you too, my little bear," I whispered. My eyes mist over with emotion. Shiloh loved it when I called him that, as his face lit up with a smile.

"The mouse is smart, Mum," he said. Still smiling.

"Yeah, Shiloh, you're smart too, right?" I asked. My heart filled with love as I studied his bright eyes. I ruffled his brown hair and kissed him on the forehead. He hesitated for a moment but eventually agreed by nodding his head. "I guess so."

I placed the bookmark between the book's pages and closed it, putting it gently on the bedside table. Shiloh looked up at me with his big almond eyes, hesitating briefly before asking, "Will you stay with me for a while, Mum?" He knew I had a lot on my mind lately, and I appreciated his request for comfort.

"Of course, honey," I replied. Dimming his bedside lamp. I laid beside him and draped my arm over his frame, feeling the rise and fall of his chest as he drifted off to sleep. Shiloh hated sleeping in complete darkness, and I had continuously reassured him that monsters only existed in books, not in real life.

As I lay there, I found the rhythmic ticking of the wall clock in the room unpleasant. But Shiloh insisted we keep it because it was a gift from Brad, Ashley's best friend. I don't like Brad. He had a reputation as a womaniser, having gone through so many wives that I'd lost count. Although I didn't like him, he loved Shiloh, and I appreciated that.

Words cannot describe my immense gratitude for Shiloh, my miracle baby. After three miscarriages within a year, I'd almost given up thoughts of having a child. But, miraculously, I became pregnant when I stopped worrying and gave in to fate. Shiloh brightened my life and brought me so much joy. Although I longed for more children, I knew Shiloh was enough for me.

I stared at his peaceful face, freckled cheeks and cherubic features, and a wave of love washed over me. I watched his contented smile slowly fade, and his breathing deepened into a soft, relaxed snoring; that was all I needed to hear. I readjusted his duvet cover and hesitated, watching the brown curls that framed his peaceful face. I allowed a small smile, dimmed his table lamp again to a soft glow and crept towards the door. A quick, fleeting look revealed the Spiderman poster. The custom-built Spiderman-shaped bed with the red-bluish and black paint was a little over the top, but I'll do anything for my boy.

I returned to the living room. Tired, I sat on the plush beige couch and ran my fingers over the sleek silver vases on the glass coffee table. The living room was dimly lit, with only a tiny table lamp casting a soft glow over the space. We opted for a calming cream colour on the walls, with a bold abstract painting in blue and green taking up most of one wall. I reminisced briefly and smiled when remembering the argument with Ashley about the paint colour. He preferred sky blue, but I leaned towards the cream. I was happy I didn't back down.

The air was quiet, and I could hear my breathing as I calmed my racing thoughts. My eyes wandered to the magazine lying on the glass coffee table before me, but I couldn't focus on the words. The impending visit to the woods preoccupied my mind. I didn't know why I agreed to that insane idea! But now that the time was creeping closer, my nerves were frayed. Being alone in the woods with nothing but my thoughts for company made me want to scream. I glanced at the Windsor clock on the wall, its ticking sounding loud in the quiet room. It was only eight o'clock, and I had four long hours to wait before leaving. The thought was suffocating, and I felt my anxiety rising. My leg tapped restlessly against the cushion, and I tried to calm myself down.

My eyes drifted towards Shiloh's door, and I hesitated briefly. *Should I check on him?* But I don't want to disturb his peaceful sleep. Glancing around the room, looking for something to distract me, my eyes fell on the painting: the colours swirl and blend, a soothing balm for my frayed nerves. Taking a deep breath, I slowed my racing heart. I wanted to lose myself in the room's peaceful atmosphere, waiting for time to pass. The room felt like a sanctuary, a refuge from the chaos of the outside world. The soft glow of the lamp, the comfortable couch, and the calming painting on the wall conspired to soothe my distressed nerves.

I woke up with a start and glanced at the clock; it was 11:45 PM. I must have slept, lulled into a deep sleep by my surroundings. Grudgingly, I stood to my feet with a yawn and stretched to infuse life into my recalcitrant bones, shaking off the grogginess that clung to my body like a heavy cloak. I strode to the hallway, slipped on my hiking boots, laced them tightly, and hoisted my knapsack over my shoulder. It was a small but sturdy bag filled with essentials like a water bottle, a penknife, and other odds and ends.

Minutes before I stepped out, every ounce of energy in my body ebbed away at the thought of walking out into the unknown. Shaking my arms and rolling my shoulders, I forced my brain to prepare for the adventure. As I stood there, feeling a growing sense of unease, I realised I was about to embark on an experience I had not fully prepared for. I quickly prayed to God for protection and strength, hoping the Lord would grant me the courage to face the unknown. With a deep breath, I steadied myself, determined not to back down now.

I should have asked Lola to come, but it was too late to change my mind. With a deep sense of resignation, I forced myself to take the first step towards the door. My heart was pounding in my chest, and I could feel the sweat beginning to build on my forehead. My mind raced with all the potential dangers that awaited me. What if I got lost and ran into some wild animals? What if I got injured and had no way of calling for help?

Staring at the stairs leading to my bedroom, I hesitated. Lola's request weighed on my mind, but I couldn't bear the thought of starting a war in Huntsville if I ignored her. Frustration welled up inside me, and I let out an involuntary yawn. I clamped my mouth shut, not wanting to wake Shiloh and blow up the mission. Despite my muddled brain and body, I made a split-second decision and tiptoed to Shiloh's room instead.

I opened his bedroom door and peered inside. The sight was heart-warming. His cherubic face looked peaceful and innocent. His duvet lay haphazardly at the foot of the bed, tempting me to tuck him in, but I resisted, realising I had to depart promptly. I tore myself away, knowing I wouldn't have the resolve to go if I lingered too long. I slipped out of the house and headed straight for the woods, my heart in my mouth. It was a dark, starless night. I shivered, more from fright rather than the cold weather.

As I approached the spot Lola had described, I heard the woods coming to life. The rustling of leaves, the chirping of crickets, and the hooting of owls filled the air. Wind whistling through the trees was eerie, sending a shiver down my spine. The occasional snap of a twig under my feet made me jump. In the distance, I heard the howling of a lone wolf, making my heart race with fear.

Strangely, the creepy sounds and the woods also had a sense of calmness. The gentle rustling of leaves in the wind and the soft hooting of the owls felt almost meditative. The stillness of the woods was a stark contrast to the chaos that had led me there. As I stood there, taking in the sounds and the serenity of the woods, I realised this venture wasn't so foolish. Perhaps this was what I needed to clear my head and find peace.

Then I remembered the reason I was there.

There was none! Lola just asked me to be here, and, I obeyed like a lamb being led to the slaughter. I thought and ground my teeth in frustration as different thoughts coursed through my mind. There can't be peace in this mysterious place. It was dark and lonely. I rubbed my hands on my face, and it took a while for my eye to get accustomed to the darkness.

Time dragged on. I contemplated returning to my comfortable bed, and that was when I saw a man darting behind a tree. He was eight meters away. My senses came alive as I watched with apprehension, my hand on the gun my dad gave me before he died. It's always with me as a safety measure.

I stood still, watching the man's movement. I noticed how he glanced around like a rabid dog. Satisfied he was alone, he whistled. Two men emerged from the shadows, dragging a bulging bag between them. I peered at my wristwatch to catch the time, but it was too dark. My mind went wild with all kinds of theories. *What are they dragging off that night? How did my best friend get a whiff of their plans?* This was wrong. It wasn't right. I felt it deep in my bones.

The cold night air wrapped around me like a second skin, sending shivers down my spine, and the thick canopy of trees made the moon barely visible, casting ghostly shadows across the forest floor. The pungent odour of decomposing leaves blended with the fragrance of moist earth. The rustling of nocturnal creatures and the occasional hoot of an owl were the only sounds that broke the silence. As I watched the men, I noticed their dishevelled appearance. Their clothes were tattered and stained, and their hair was unkempt. The man who whistled had a scar above his eyebrow, making him appear menacing. I was proud of my night eye; spotting a scar that far away was no mean feat, yet I couldn't see the time on my watch, it was blurry. The other two were hefty men, with arms that looked like tree trunks. I cursed my short-sightedness. I wished I'd taken my reading glasses.

They got to a secluded spot and began to dig. I held my breath for a few seconds and expelled the air from my lungs. It felt like someone was strangling me, and I gasped for breath. I merged with the trees, praying they wouldn't notice me. Tears trickled down my cheeks when I realised I was witnessing a crime. A voice kept screaming for me to leave the scene, but I couldn't. Fear glued my feet to the spot. I watched with dismay, and bile rose in my throat. The more the three men ploughed into the soft soil, the more my anger and frustration grew.

Their boots were making an annoying crunching sound, and then an idea dropped into my mind like dew from heaven. I thought of ways to surprise them. Shooting into the air and hoping they bailed out? Call the police? The more I contemplated the option, the more I saw myself joining whosoever they buried in that shallow grave. I watched the men and noticed the determined Jaws. They looked ferocious enough to overpower me, so I discarded the idea outright. I thought of Shiloh alone in the house, and I gritted my teeth in frustration. My son sleeping alone in the house overwhelmed me with fear I wanted to scream.

What were the odds of his life being in danger? What if someone saw me when I left my house? My sweaty palms showed my growing panic, and I regretted putting my son in harm's way, but moving away from my position was not wise. If I did, I would be playing with death.

"Don't put the cart before the horse," I heard Mum's voice. If she were with me now, she would advise me to think things through before rushing to a decision, but as usual, the warnings went unheeded, and I dashed back to her when I'd made a fool of myself again.

Mum supported me, even when she knew I was wrong. She was at my beck and call until her dying day, and I blamed her for overindulging me while growing up. My clumsiness and inability to make quick decisions were the banes of my life, and the only day I decided to be quick with my choices, I ended up putting the life of my only son in danger. I have a good heart; there was no doubt about that, but was that enough in a world filled with unimaginable dangers? I wouldn't deliberately hurt a fellow human being.

My mind went back to the unfolding scene. *Who was the victim? Were the men involved in the murder?* My hands shook as I clutched my gun, wondering if I should confront them or call the police. Fear and anger bubbled inside me, and I knew I had to do something. But my legs felt like they were made of stone. I couldn't move.

A familiar scent wafted through the darkness, and my heart stopped for a microsecond. All thoughts of my mother were forgotten in a flash as my breathing came in a short, panicked gasp. I froze when I saw a recognisable figure between *the three wicked* men as I had code-named them. I rubbed my eyes twice, staring at the huge, tall man talking in hushed tones with the men. He was the fourth man. I didn't notice when he arrived. He walked with a swagger. The scent of my homemade clothes softener gave him away. The characteristic neck cracking also hit a cord in my cold heart. Only two people in the world used my conditioner, and they lived in my house. Besides, Ashley enjoyed cracking his neck even though he knew I found it repulsive, but he didn't care anyway, and I'd stopped complaining. My heart sank when I realised it was him, all right.

"What am I going to do?" I asked no one in particular, and my heart broke into fragments. I gawked in horror as Ashley strode away from the men in easy strides. I couldn't control myself any longer.

'Oh my Lord, what am I going to do?' I repeated in agony. I knew I didn't have answers to my questions, nor did I expect any reply. My entire world just became a hellhole.

Ashley is, on second thoughts, I should probably describe him as *'was'* in the past tense. With an ashen face, I realised the man I vowed to spend the rest of my life with was a criminal. I stared at my expensive wedding ring, and an insane rage built up in me. I swallowed hard for the umpteenth time. *How did my husband fit in with murderers? How on earth would he explain this?* Burying a human being was probably the worst sin of all.

My brother would have a field day at my expense if this got out, finding absolute pleasure in the scandal that would ensue. I closed my eyes and leaned on the tree that had become my refuge. My problems were far more than the snarling, harsh rebuke that may be unleashed on me by my hateful brother rather than the awful realisation that I was in a very precarious situation. I had to use restraint and wisdom. But I couldn't shake the feeling of trepidation and the nagging fear that the whole town probably knew of the antics of my murderous husband. The police will haunt me, knocking on my door regardless of my philanthropic deeds. After all, bad news has a pungent odour and travelled far.

Ashley, an aeronautics engineer, had a strong presence with his impressive looks. He had a unique mix of races that made him intriguing. His warm, tan skin showed he loved being outdoors. His brown eyes could express a lot, going from dark to a lighter honey-brown. His thick, wavy brown hair framed his face nicely, and he often ran his hands through it, which only made him more appealing. Despite his rugged appearance, there was a softness in his expression that drew me in. Thanks to his dedication to exercise, he was in great shape, especially when he wasn't travelling for work. His broad shoulders gave him a commanding presence, and his irresistible energy effortlessly drew people towards him.

We met at an auction house in downtown Los Angeles and instantly hit it off. My brother, Henry, didn't approve and told me straight up that he thought Ashley was a player who would hurt me. He predicted Ashley would break my heart. But by then, I was already head over heels in love. That was the end of the story. Twelve weeks later, we got married.

Looking back, I can't help but realise that, despite our differences, my brother was spot on about Ashley's true character.

I wasn't worried about our wedding day when I saw an array of strange faces I never saw again. None of Ashley's family made the trip from South Africa. It didn't bother me. When I asked about their conspicuous absence, Ashley explained it was short notice and that we'd travel to Pretoria after our honeymoon. Even though the revelation hurled my super-suspicious friend off balance, Lola never said a word against him. I knew she disapproved of 'us', but Ashley was the type of man who left a lasting impression, one that stayed with you long after he was gone; whether that impression was suspicion or adoration, I couldn't tell but I fell in love with him, and that was it.

I wasn't perturbed either that Ashley lived in a hotel throughout our brief courtship or that he knew practically everything there was to know about my family and me.

And about my in-laws, I reckoned I would meet them in time even though I never did... yet.

Like every love story, mine also had hiccups. Ashley's constant trips to New York had grated on my nerves. His usual excuse was work, because he wouldn't rely on me for every dollar we needed. I explained to him we didn't need the money; Mother left me millions in the bank. We need not work a day if we don't want to, and we'd still be comfortable, but I respected Ashley for his decision. I couldn't always have my way, which was probably one of the hardest lessons in a marriage. It's all about compromise and suppressing your needs for the greater good, not that I believe in that ideology.

Earlier that morning, before he left home, he'd told me his company was sending him to New York for a two-day conference. Our sex life was great, but I sensed it was as if he was miles away when we were together. It was a weird feeling, but I couldn't shake it off. When we kissed, there was a longing look on his face. I remembered flashing him my sexiest smile, hoping he'd understand and take me back into the bedroom because I wanted him to stay, but as usual, I hid under my perfect housewife mode and allowed him to go.

He'd kissed Shiloh on the forehead and left the house. I refused to see him off, a sign I wasn't happy with his frequent trips to New York. It was pathetic that my only form of protest was not seeing him at the door. I was sure Lola would have scoffed at my naivety.

I heard a buzzing sound in my left ear and slapped my ear so hard the men stopped digging and glanced in my direction. I grated my teeth and sucked in my breath, and came to the unpleasant conclusion they have discovered me! My breathing became shallow and quick, and my palms were slick with sweat. I felt like a hunted animal, waiting for the predator to pounce. It was time for me to call it a day by taking to my heels, and I did as a brilliant light beamed on me.

I ran as hard and fast as possible, thankful for my frequent walks with Shiloh. I knew the pathways well; it was permanently etched in my brain. I fled, darting in between trees with my hands making a juggling motion. Darkness was like a light before me as I ran, and the smell of impending rain lifted my spirits. I ran through the forest like a deer. I must have lost them because there was no sound of pounding feet gaining hard after me, and then I slowed down for a while to catch my breath, even though I felt cornered and frightened.

I walked the rest of the journey home, glancing at the friendless black sky, my mind in disarray. A rumble of thunder jolted me back to the present, and the air smelled of impending rain. I heaved a deep sigh of relief when my house appeared before me, but my head was still in a daze. I've been living with a monster. What if Ashley attacked us? How can I protect my son and myself? The thought of the gun gave me a respite, and I'll use it to defend us if need be. I hopped on the steps and shuffled to the front door with shaky hands.

A slight draft made the curtains in the living room flutter, and I saw the kitchen door ajar. My hand was on the doorknob with the house key, but something made me pause. Panic crept up my spine like icy fingers, and I clenched my teeth and pushed them down. I couldn't afford to scream and draw attention. Not with my son upstairs, sleeping soundly, oblivious to the danger lurking in our home.

My mind raced as I remembered Lola's strange behaviour earlier. She knew about the murder too, but why was she so afraid to tell me the complete story? How did she find out about their plans? *Seeing is believing,* a voice whispered in my head.

Three men were burying a body, my husband among them. The weight of their secrets and the burden of my knowledge weighed on me. The thought of being an accessory to murder sickened me, but I couldn't ignore the crime. Reporting it meant I would implicate my husband and destroy our family. I want a happy home for Shiloh, I've seen what broken marriages do to children, and I don't want my son to grow up in one.

How desperate are you Christine? I thought, sad at how my life was crumbling around me. I found myself with no power or ability to act and felt completely helpless.

Thoughts swirled through my mind as I considered my options. I shook my head in despair and put my key into the lock, turning it gently. The door opened slowly with a creak. I entered, locked the front door, put the key in my pocket, and leaned on the door for a minute. The house was eerily quiet, the kind of dissonant silence that makes you feel uneasy.

As I struggled with my conscience, I noticed the silence in the house—no sounds of my husband or anyone else. My heart pounded in my chest, and my breath came in short gasps as I tiptoed towards the kitchen door. With my hand on the doorknob, I took a deep breath and pushed the door open.

The darkness swallowed me, and I strained to hear any sound. A shuffling sound jolted me out of my passive state, but I restrained myself and waited, merging with the darkness, and then I peered outside. Everywhere was quiet, although I was shaking with dread. I thought of calling Lola. After all, she was the one who sent me on the ill-fated mission that resulted in my being hunted down like an outlaw. But calling her was a bad idea. She would be asleep, and I shelved the idea.

Suddenly, a crack of thunder accompanied by lightning illuminated the kitchen and the garden. I saw the silhouette of someone and wasn't sure if it was the shadow of a man or a woman. Pretending to be oblivious to the intruder, I closed the door as quietly as possible while my mind raced for a solution. My son's life was in danger if I didn't act fast, and I'm determined to fight for him with the last drop of my blood. I considered using the gun, but the past few hours taught me it wasn't a wise decision. I don't care about myself anymore; my only thought was for the safety of Shiloh. I found inner strength with the idea of what might happen if I did nothing, and I didn't want to imagine a worst-case scenario.

I walked to the kitchen sink, and my heartbeat increased in crescendo. I saw what I was looking for, but was too slow. When I turned around, the last sound I heard was the heavy rain falling outside the kitchen window, and there was pitch darkness.

PART TWO

THE FINAL SILENCE

As I regained consciousness, I felt a throbbing pain in my head, and my vision was blurred. My attempts to move were unsuccessful. My body felt heavy and uncooperative. Panic set in when I realised I did not know where I was or how I got there. A beautiful arrangement of lavender and rose flowers in a white vase caught my eye, along with get-well cards neatly arranged in a drawer beside the bed.

My eyes hurt, and a weak groan escaped me. I checked my surroundings. I was in a clean, sterile room painted turquoise blue. The room was lit with a fluorescent bulb flickering in the ceiling, casting a cold and clinical light on everything. The bed was positioned close to the wall, and my heart raced, accompanied by tingling feet. It was the onset of a panic attack. Besides, my skin itched if I didn't sleep on my crisp Egyptian cotton bedsheets.

Egyptian cotton sheets.

Why Egyptian cotton sheets? I thought and moved to check and saw white sheets tightly tucked in. Not Egyptian. *It doesn't matter anymore;* I thought sadly. I moved my elevated head on a pile of pillows and felt a jarring, throbbing pain. Exhaling deeply, I took repeated, deep breaths to calm my racing heart.

I noticed an IV bag hung from a metal stand nearby, and the rhythmic beeps of the heart monitor provided a reassuring sound in the room. I felt dizzy, and my eyes trailed to the far side of the wall. A small window, or what was it, two? I couldn't focus, but realised I needed to know where I was. The window let in a sliver of sunlight, illuminating the dust particles floating in the air. My eyes followed the dust, and I heard the hubbub of voices floating in through the window. Cars started, revving and driving off, a cacophony of noises that screamed life. I liked the sound of life and activities. The dead can't work, or talk, or cry.

"That must be the car park," I intoned. My voice was hoarse, and my parched throat struggled with each sound. I imagined the bleak weather and struggling trees in the concrete parking, facing the scorching Alabama sun. My attention returned to the room, fixating on the table beside the bed. A pitcher of water and a plastic cup sat there, untouched, accompanied by a stack of magazines and books. I longed to rummage through one of them, but the weight on my head discouraged me from making sudden movements. It was like an oppressive burden that threatened to send me crashing to the floor.

Suddenly, another sound caught my attention. In the corner of the room, mounted on the wall, a television played daytime talk shows and news programs. Newsreaders with heavy makeup and flashing pearly white teeth smiled on cue. The low volume of the TV combined with the beeping monitor intensified the atmosphere. And it hit me.

I'm in solitary confinement in a prison hospital! The thought frightened me until I noticed the intravenous drip attached to my left arm. It became apparent that I was indeed in a hospital. But why would I be in prison? I shook my head at my confusion, but the weight on my shoulders stifled my movements, causing a groan to escape my parched lips. I tried to recall the last few hours of my life, but my memory failed me. However, one image loomed large in my mind.

Shiloh.

Where's my son? I thought in fear, my eyes darting everywhere, sweat gathered on my forehead and my mouth felt dry.

As my rapid breathing subsided, I took a deep breath and closed my eyes. I hyperventilated, and in my mind, I heard my mother's voice – or rather, her voice as I remembered it. You know how it is. *"Calm down, Kitty; you'll be alright."* Her voice had a magical way of soothing me, and I cherished the nickname she gave me. There was a story behind that name, a tale of its own.

But the mystery of how I ended up in the hospital remained unsolved. I hadn't pondered for long when a nurse entered the room, wearing a bright smile. Her teeth spar-kled white, and her perfume permeated the air, filling the room with a pleasant scent. I liked her.

"Good afternoon, Mrs White. You gave us quite a fright. How are you feeling?" She greeted me cheerfully.

"Not good," I mumbled, struggling to focus on her beau-tiful face as something blurred my vision.

"What happened?" I asked. I found it challenging to keep my head upright. Speaking was a Herculean task as if I were carrying a concrete slab on my shoulders.

"Someone hit you on the head with a bottle of wine. The cops are investigating the attack," the nurse replied, main-taining her smile but carrying a knowing look that suggested she knew more than she was letting on.

"Your husband and son are outside. Would you like to see them now? It's visiting time," she informed me before leaving the room. I nodded, apprehensive about what I should say to Ashley. Suddenly, memories of that dreadful night flooded my mind, and a wave of horror washed over me.

Ashley and Shiloh entered the room, causing my heart to skip a beat. My dry lips quivered with fear, and I yearned for a drink.

"Hi, Mum! I missed you!" Shiloh exclaimed with de-light, rushing into my open arms, and planting a wet kiss on my cheek. He handed me a small homemade card, and I held him close, not wanting to let go. I examined the card with pictures of me, noticing how he had drawn me slightly larger than life. Seeing him brought immense joy to my heart.

"Thank you, love," I murmured, shifting my attention to Ashley, who stood back, staring at me with an unreadable expression. There was an intensity in his demeanour. He clenched and unclenched his fist, pressing his lips together in a sneer. Without saying a word, I knew he was upset and struggling to maintain a blank face. The events of the past few weeks were a testament to that. I was married to a stranger.

"Hello, darling," he said after Shiloh gave him a disapproving glare, and kissed me on the forehead. His upper lip remained stiff, as if sculpted from granite.

"Christine, everyone in town has heard of your foolish escapade with that conniving woman!" Ashley exploded in anger, his expression filled with hatred. I sensed the tension from his broad shoulders, and his expressive brown eyes betrayed his concern. Beneath his tightly clenched jaw, rage smouldered, and he struggled to maintain control over his emotions. He didn't care that Shiloh was present. We had agreed never to quarrel in front of him. I wondered how such a handsome man could be so problematic. His striking features were captivating and intimidating, and those who crossed his path did so at their peril. Ashley frightened me that night in the woods, and now I had to choose my words carefully. But, as usual, I didn't think things through.

"What the hell are you talking about?" I shouted, and I regretted my outburst because my head felt like a volcano about to erupt, and I groaned in pain. Shiloh looked worried.

"Dad, please call the doctor," he pleaded, his voice breaking into a whisper, fading like distant thunder during a storm. Ashley glared at his son and stormed out of the room.

"Mum, it was Dad!" Shiloh screamed, lowering his voice to a conspiratorial tone when Ashley was out of earshot. His misty eyes were red, and his tiny chest heaved with emotion. Tears threatened to spill at any moment.

"What are you saying, darling?" I asked. My heart was pounding so fiercely that it was audible.

Shiloh nodded his head, willing me to believe him. He continued in the same quiet voice. "That night, I couldn't sleep, Mum. There was a crack of lightning close to my window. The sound woke me up, and when I checked your room, you weren't there. I thought you were in the kitchen, so I came down. I saw Dad hitting you on the head."

Shiloh's voice trembled as he spoke, tears streaming down his face, "I was so scared, Mum. I didn't know what to do."

My heart shattered into a million pieces at the thought of what my son had witnessed. He buried his face in my chest, sobbing. "I was scared to stop him because he was so angry and didn't even notice me," he said.

I held him tightly, attempting to comfort him. "It's okay, darling. You did the right thing by telling me. I'm so proud of you for being brave." But deep inside, rage and disbelief consumed me. How could Ashley do this to me? To our son? We had problems, but I never imagined he would stoop so low.

"Are you sure, dear? You're not dreaming?" I asked again. Although I already knew the truth. Shiloh continued to sob and I cradled him in my arms, disregarding the throbbing pain in my head. Footsteps echoed down the hallway, signalling the approach of someone. He moved away from my embrace, wiping the tears from his face with the back of his hands, but his eyes remained red, and upon closer inspection, anyone could tell that something had upset him.

"Don't say a word to anyone, okay?" I whispered into his ear, and he nodded, still frightened. I longed to embrace him again and chase away all his fears, but knew I couldn't risk arousing suspicion. I needed to be strong for us and assure Shiloh I would get stronger and uncover the truth about the monster I married. For once, I needed to take responsibility for my life instead of burdening it on someone else's shoulders. There was no excuse for Ashley's actions. He had no right to strike me, no matter the circumstances, and Shiloh had witnessed it. I knew our marriage was over, but I couldn't fathom what lay ahead. My duty now was to protect my son and myself from further harm.

A doctor entered the hospital room, accompanied by Ashley. Thankfully, the hours turned into days as I endured countless tests and CT scans. Fortunately, there was no brain damage. The linear skull fracture from the attack was healing, and my progress was satisfactory. There was no bleed in my brain and no other intervention was necessary.

Two weeks later, the doctors deemed me well enough to be discharged.

***

Lola's visit on the day of my return caused an unsettling feeling in me. Her strange behaviour, lack of eye contact, and small talk about the weather and my upcoming birthday made me uneasy. Something was off, leaving me with an unsettling sense of apprehension. As we sat in my living room, sipping our coffee, I could no longer bear the suffocating weight of uncertainty. I confronted her.

"Why did you tell me to go to the woodland that night? How did you know about everything?" I blurted out, my heart thundering in my chest.

The silence that followed was deafening, pregnant with the weight of untold secrets. Lola appeared lost in her thoughts, grappling with the words to divulge. But I'd run out of patience. My life teetered on the edge of destruction, and I refused to be a mere pawn in a sinister game, an accessory to murder, depending on who or what Ashley and his friends were burying.

"I'm going to the police. I'll tell them everything I know. You can't keep me in the dark any longer. I nearly lost my life!" I wailed. The sheer terror of the situation coursing through my veins. "I could have died, Lola," I whimpered, collapsing to the floor, overwhelmed by emotions. She rushed to my side, her embrace offering solace, but her silence spoke volumes. Seconds stretched into minutes as we clung to each other until she pulled away, a troubled expression fixed on her face.

"Ashley made advances towards me," she spoke with an unnerving calmness. Her eyes hardened, her mouth forming a tight line. "He wanted to violate me on the day Shiloh was born before we both came to see you at the hospital..."

I was struck dumb by her revelation, first Shiloh and now Lola. *My own Ashley? The man I trusted with my life! He'd transformed into a monster, from an unconfirmed murderer to a sexual predator. What should I do?* I thought as fear and disbelief washed over me, mingling with a profound sense of betrayal. I sank back onto the sofa, deflated, while Lola knelt beside me, pressing a tender kiss into my trembling hands. She stared into my eyes for a long, silent moment, radiating a love that transcended words.

"I love you, Christine, even when you act foolish and blind to the truth," she chuckled, her voice laced with genuine affection. "Perhaps, for once, your brother Henry was right. Ashley is a fraud. We've met none of his supposed family. It's been one excuse after another. Wake up, my friend. Leave him before it's too late."

"I can't," I whispered, my voice choked with despair, "Shiloh needs a father."

"And you both need to be safe," Lola whispered, her voice laced with concern as she searched my eyes, pleading for understanding. "Your life is in danger here," she continued, her brows furrowed with worry. "Did you sign a prenuptial agreement?"

"Ashley doesn't care about my inheritance. He has a stable job," I replied, the defensive tone creeping into my voice, but still tinged with lingering doubt. Notwithstanding the revelations, a part of me still clung to the remnants of the life I had built with him. After all, he hadn't been unkind to me or Shiloh until the incident in the woodland.

"But he desired your best friend," a voice screamed within me, challenging my fragile loyalty.

"Did you sleep with him?" I asked, desperation tainting my words, praying for a denial.

"Not even if he were the last man on Earth," Lola retorted indignantly. "Who do you take me for? Do you honestly think I would betray you? You take me for a home wrecker?" Lola fired the fusillades of questions at me, and I saw the pain in her eyes.

"I apologise," I interjected, feeling relief and guilt wash over me. "But you haven't truly answered my question. You've only danced around it."

"Yes, I know," Lola acknowledged, her expression grave.

She rose from her kneeling position and settled onto the opposite sofa, her behaviour impenetrable and troubled. A stray lock of hair framed her face, and she brushed it away. Her husband, a skilled surgeon, adored her. What more could she desire? Frustration rose within me, battling against the swirling doubts and uncertainties clouding my mind.

"I want to know everything, Lola," I pleaded, my voice laced with desperation.

"I know," she sighed, her gaze distant, as if lost memories. "But you need to hear it from Ashley himself. I happened to be in the right place at the right time and overheard a conversation in a grocery store. I was in the adjacent aisle when I recognised your husband's voice."

She shrugged her shoulders, her expression impenetrable. "Maybe he was speaking to his friends, or maybe not. But I heard every word. The details are hazy, but the implications were clear. Then, you entered the picture. I can't say more, Christine. I'm sorry."

"Thank you," I murmured, the weight of her words settling upon me. "I think it's time I go to the police."

She nodded in silent agreement, and as if on cue, the sound of Ashley's sleek Mercedes Benz echoed through the driveway. With a hurried excuse about running errands for her sister, Lola jumped on her feet, and I escorted her to the door and watched as she sprinted to her car, gave Ashley a quick wave, jumped into her Range, and gunned it out of our driveway. I returned to the living room, pacing up and down like a woman in labour. I was steeling myself for the impending confrontation. Shiloh was away, enjoying a sleepover with a friend, providing the perfect opportunity for a long-overdue conversation with Ashley.

Lola's revelation left me reeling. Ashley was not who I thought he was. It was unbelievable, but deep down, I knew Lola would not lie about something like this. If a man could bury a human being deep in the woods at midnight, I don't think there's any redemption left in him. I needed to confront Ashley and hear his side of the story.

As he entered the room, I sensed his tension. A guarded expression had replaced his usual bright and cheerful face, and the unspoken weight of the atmosphere hung heavy in the air.

I prepared his dinner, awaiting the right moment to confront him. After eating, he moved away from the dining table and slumped onto the sofa, his face devoid of emotion. I paced back and forth, grappling with my nerves, but just as I summoned the courage to speak, he stood up, dropped the remote control on the sofa, and grabbed his car keys from the centre table.

"I'm going to Chad's house," he announced.

"To bury another corpse, I presume," I retorted with hands on my hips, my head throbbing with the anguish of betrayal and Lola's revelations. The pain pulsed with an unforgiving intensity, but I knew I had to confront him. The words came out with bitterness and anger, fuelled by the suspicion eating away at me.

"Excuse me? What in the world are you talking about?" he yelled, staring at me as if I'd lost my mind.

"Don't play innocent! I saw you with three men burying a body on the night an intruder attacked me!" I screamed, my pent-up emotions bursting forth unchecked. My need for answers and the truth eclipsed the fear of his potential rage.

His face turned pale, and a wicked glint flickered in his brown eyes. He glared at me with a chilling coldness, and the brewing rage in his towering physique sent a chill coursing through my soul. *Is he going to kill me?* I wondered frantically. I'm petite, five inches over five feet, while Ashley stood over six feet tall and weighed over seventeen stone. He could snuff out my life with a single blow.

I watched him in silence, my every instinct attuned to his every move. He closed his eyes, and when they reopened, he took a step closer, looming over me. Anticipating a physical confrontation, my body stiffened, and I instinctively stepped back.

"That must have been my doppelgänger because I was in New York..." he said with a hint of sarcasm and then paused, his features softening. He avoided eye contact, his mood swinging. My heart raced as I waited for him to continue. I steeled myself for the inevitable and the look in his eyes confirmed my suspicions. Part of me dreaded hearing his words, but I knew I had to uncover the truth. I braced for the impact of his words.

"I was having an affair," he confessed, avoiding eye contact.

The words hit me like a tidal wave. It was a confession, but not the one I'd expected. I struggled to comprehend what Ashley had revealed. At that moment, everything changed, and I knew I would never be the same. I'd been a fool to think he would admit to murder. Who was I kidding? But it was him, and he'd even seduced my friend. The man I thought I knew had become a stranger before my eyes.

What about my attacker? My son does not lie. He's my boy, innocent. *The assailant could have been anyone,* a voice whispered in my mind. I swallowed hard, studying him intently.

A few seconds later, my voice hoarse, I mustered the courage to ask, "Do you love her?"

Ashley's eyes turned icy, and the painful truth unfolded before me. The man I married had become unrecognisable. Tremors coursed through my body, like the numbing coldness that seeps into my bones during winter. In a flash, my life up until that moment raced before my eyes. I was a carefree full-time housewife raised by a single mother who never remarried after my father's death when I was fourteen. Even though there was no shortage of suitors, she'd chosen to focus on raising me and my brother, who had become a successful Wall Street broker. And what about me? I managed the numerous estates my mother left behind. I had left the endless partying in New York, embraced my faith, got closer to God, and transformed into an ordinary Huntsville housewife. Knowing the truth about Ashley's involvement in a murder and his affair has not affected my feelings for him. I still loved him and would do anything to keep my family together.

But deep down, I'm no fool and know the reality facing me. In the depths of the woodlands, the lifeless remains of our marriage lay buried, its demise sealed on that fateful night. Yet, I clutched desperately at straws, unwilling to let go. What kind of woman does that?

A rational voice inside me screamed, *"Your marriage died in the woodlands that fateful night. Why are you still clinging to hope?"* I looked around and would give anything for Lola to be with me now. But there are some battles you fight alone. This was one of them.

"I don't know, darling. I love you and Shiloh, but you have become elusive and aloof, and I've been lonely," Ashley said with hunched shoulders, cutting a picture of pity. Tears welled in my eyes as he stood before me, his once-loving eyes now tenuous and indifferent. Loneliness had enveloped our relationship, leaving me yearning for connection. But deep down, I knew better than to trust him. He casually sat back on the sofa, content with his feeble excuses, as if they could mend our shattered trust.

My hands fell limp at my sides, my heart heavy with guilt. "Baby, if only you'd told me how you truly felt," I whispered, frantically seeking a way out of the wreckage that was my marriage. As an eternal optimist, I believed we could still salvage what was left.

But Ashley rose to his feet again, his gaze filled with sorrow. With finality lacing his words, he uttered the words that crushed my soul: "I want a divorce, Christine. I'm leaving for New York. Even Jesus acknowledged divorce in the face of adultery."

His tone left no room for negotiation. It was over. Yet my tenacious spirit refused to accept defeat. I couldn't bear the thought of losing Ashley or giving up on our marriage. I clung to a flicker of hope.

Desperate, I cried out, my voice filled with love and anguish. "I'll never leave you, Ashley. I love you."

I reached out to touch him, longing for that connection we once shared, but he flinched away, escaping my grasp.

The gravity of his decision etched deep lines of sorrow on his face. I had lost him. I despised the feeling of losing, but I had lost everything—my friends and my family's support. Even my brother had distanced himself since our marriage. Everyone seemed to be against Ashley. Yet, I remained loyal, standing by his side.

Trying to understand his motives, I asked softly, trembling, "Are you in trouble with the law?"

The curtness of his reply sent shivers down my spine. "No," he answered, his eyes devoid of emotion, staring right through me. Confusion gripped my heart as I desperately sought answers.

"Then why? Why are you so determined to ruin your life?"

"Just give me what I want, Christine. Shiloh can stay with you," he pleaded.

"Have you killed before?"

"Stop interrogating me, or you'll regret it!" he screamed, kicking his feet like a tantrum-throwing toddler. I had struck a nerve.

Frustrated by my persistent questioning, Ashley's anger scared me, his tantrum reminiscent of a petulant child. I retreated to our room, hastily locking the door in fear for my safety. My heart pounded against my chest, threatening to burst with each beat. I knew I needed to regain control over my emotions lest they consume me entirely. With trembling hands, I pulled out my phone, instinctively activating the voice recorder. Whatever was to happen between us, I needed to document it.

Looking at my reflection in the dressing table's mirror, I saw a woman drowning in sorrow. My tear-filled eyes shone brightly, and my cheeks flushed with turmoil. I took a deep breath, exhaling slowly, trying to steady myself. I had to believe that I could handle this storm. I clung to the fragments of our shattered love, praying that Ashley would grant us a second chance. Perhaps, deep down, he would find the courage to surrender himself to the authorities. But in the chaos, a nagging thought invaded my mind. What about the soul lost in those haunting woodlands? Shouldn't justice prevail?

With each passing moment, my thoughts remained fixated on a glimmer of hope, no matter how distant it seemed. I had no idea that unravelling the web of lies would take me on a suspenseful and treacherous journey. Every step I took in pursuit of the truth would expose chilling revelations that would forever alter the course of my life.

I opened the door and stepped outside, my heart pounding with intensity. Ashley stood at the foot of the stairs, his bright brown eyes locking onto mine – the very eyes that once captured my heart. But now, there was a sense of sadness, and every breath I took felt like a dagger to my soul.

"I've made a decision, Christine," he said, his voice trembling. "I still love you, but I had an affair. When I tried to end it, she refused, and in the ensuing struggle, I killed her. It wasn't premeditated, Christine. It was a horrible accident." A heavy silence hung in the air as Ashley confirmed my worst fears. Taking a deep breath, he stepped forward and planted his right foot on the stairs. I watched him closely, my hand finding the stair rail.

"There's a darkness within me that I can't control or erase," he continued, "but my love for you was real. I truly loved you, Christine."

Time ceased as we stared at each other, emotions raging between us. Part of me wanted to believe him, to rush into his arms and assure him everything would be okay. But doubts and questions gnawed at me. What if he was being manipulated? What if there were other reasons behind the murder? Could telling me the complete truth put us in danger? What if, against all odds, Ashley was innocent?

"You have to believe me," he pleaded, barely whispering. "But I've destroyed everything. I asked Chad and his two friends for help that night, but your friend Lola saw us, so we had to cancel and reschedule. I had already given Chad a hundred thousand dollars. He had to uphold his end of the deal," his voice trailed off.

I clutched my phone tightly to my chest, feeling my heart smashed into countless pieces. Ashley loved me! But as I watched him, my hair stood on end and my knees knocked together. My heartbeat increased in intensity because of fear even though I loved him. I watched as he struggled to gather his thoughts. Several seconds later, he mustered the courage to continue.

"We buried her that night, making sure you thought I was in New York. Sadie Newton was *just a bar girl*, but we'd be in prison if we didn't silence her. I'm so sorry, Christine. Please forgive me. I can't go back to prison." His words left me reeling. Was Sadie just a bar girl? And what did he mean by not going back to prison? Ashley had never been to jail, so what did he mean by not returning?

So many conflicting thoughts raced through my head, causing unbearable pain.

Ashley's mournful eyes rested on mine. Begging for forgiveness, I yearned to embrace him and tell him none of it mattered. But something held me back, and I remained frozen on the landing, unable to speak. Minutes stretched on, lost in his tearful eyes, praying for a way out of this nightmare he'd created.

Finally finding my voice, I whispered, "I still love you," grasping for a solution. We could escape to non-extradition countries and start anew. But Sadie's family deserved answers, and her life mattered too. I couldn't bear the thought of Shiloh buried in a shallow grave like Sadie. The guilt weighed heavily on me, and I despised myself for being in this impossible position. As a Christian, I knew I should report Ashley to the authorities, but I felt paralysed, unable to act. I prayed for strength and wisdom.

His sorrowful eyes met mine, and their pain tore at my heart. He attempted to smile, but his words were barely audible, "I attacked you in the kitchen because I knew you saw me that night, and I was terrified. I'm a killer, darling, and the state would execute me. I can't face Sadie's parents or live with this guilt any longer." Before I could react, his hand moved to his head, and I lunged down the stairs, but it was too late.

The deafening sound of the gunshot echoed through the air, a high-pitched shriek echoing in the surroundings.

PART THREE

SECRETS UNRAVELLED

Three harrowing weeks had dragged on since the tragic death of Ashley, and I was still numb with shock. There were emotions I had to plough through, from anger and betrayal to fear and grief, and some I couldn't even put a finger on yet. I struggled with so much anxiety that it tightened its suffocating grip around my heart, refusing to release its hold. Ashley's absence was unfathomable; I couldn't accept that he was gone. Devil or angel, I was married to him for almost ten years. Lola, never one to sugarcoat her words, relentlessly reminded me I should be relieved to be rid of a confessed murderer rather than wallowing in sorrow. But Ashley was more than a husband to me—he embodied my deepest love, the essence of my existence. I mourned the loss of an image I'd built on lies, a phantom marriage. I still assumed we would be lifelong partners, bound by an unbreakable bond. But now, it felt as if I were stuck in a never-ending nightmare where the horrors refused to cease, and it all started that fateful night in the woods. I felt drained and hollow. The truth of that unfortunate incident lingered, haunting my every waking moment. It felt like my past had trapped me in an alternate, twisted reality that refused to dissipate. Ashley's suicide exacerbated my anguish, a never-ending roller-coaster of pain and sorrow.

Henry, my eccentric brother, has mysteriously vanished while pursuing elusive business deals in London. He didn't need the money. Leaving just a voicemail after hearing about Ashley's death was difficult to accept. He hinted at the possibility of permanently moving to the United Kingdom, which could mean we won't see each other for a long time. We weren't close as siblings because of our indifference and distance. It mattered little to me where he wandered off to. He could vanish into the depths of Timbuktu for all I cared! But his indirect communication hurt me deeply, reminding me of how much I needed him. There was a part of me that craved a connection with my blood relatives. Apart from Shiloh, Henry was the only living link to my lineage—a fragile lifeline in an uncertain world. While I loved Lola, a part of me silently longed for the restoration of familial ties, a chance to bridge the chasms created by my ill-fated union with Ashley.

Brad and two of Ashley's close friends came to offer their condolences, but their presence brought no comfort, only an uneasy feeling. Our family lawyer, Alistair Chaplain, was a tall and forbidding figure with a face devoid of warmth approached me where I sat. I stood up and asked him to follow me to the kitchen. Without saying anything, he gave me a nondescript brown envelope. The tremor in my hands gave away my apprehension as I carefully tore open the envelope, revealing a letter with the ominous phrase "Tales of five lies". Overwhelmed by confusion and desperation, I turned to the lawyer for answers.

Alistair's bloodshot eyes never left mine as he revealed the deceit surrounding Ashley. He told me Ashley wanted me to know the truth if anything happened to him. My heart stopped beating for a second, and my mouth turned dry. The reality of my marital relationship with Ashley had been different. I was living in a fantasy, a life built on lies and deception. My husband, whom I still endearingly call 'beloved' in my thoughts, turned out to be a sly serial bigamist engaged in multiple illicit relationships. Four wives, six children, scattered across three states—each an unsuspecting victim, and I, the fifth wife. My precious child, Shiloh, serves as a haunting reminder of Ashley's abnormal capacity for deceit. How sad things have become!

Time stood still, my heart arrested, as this revelation threatened to crush me. An impenetrable mask covered my face, but I cried in agony inside. It felt as if a brutal blow had seared through the core of my being and left me reeling. The professed love that Ashley had whispered, the vows exchanged under false pretences—everything shattered instantly. Betrayal was carved deep into my soul, humiliation scarred my spirit, and heartbreak consumed me whole. The weight of this revelation threatened to crush me, a vice tightening around my heart, squeezing the breath from my lungs. The lawyer's words reverberated through my being like an avalanche, and with a primal cry of anguish, I surrendered to the agony that engulfed me.

At that devastating moment, Lola, my trusted friend, extended her hand, leading me away from the frightening stare of the lawyer into the safety of my room. In the privacy of my room, I crumbled upon the bed, tears mingling with embers of dead dreams. The world as I knew it had crumbled, leaving behind a desolate landscape of broken promises and stolen trust. My mind was a jumble of conflicting thoughts. Attempting to grasp the unfortunate events leading up to the funeral, the distant echoes of Shiloh's laughter floated up to me—a fragile glimmer of hope emerged from the chaos. Regardless of my pain, at least someone in my life found solace. I clutched onto that and knew life still has meaning.

Ashley's true nature flashed in my mind, and I regretted ignoring the warning signs and unsettling feeling that came with his presence. How had I been so stupid? So oblivious to the darkness lurking within him? The marriages he planned on a foundation of deceit, the lives he destroyed with calculated precision—a murderer in every sense of the word—poor Sadie, forever trapped in the clutches of his insidious plans.

While sifting through the jumble of emotions, a haunting sense of despair settled within me. A gnawing unease, as if some vital piece of the puzzle still eluded my grasp. How had Ashley managed such deception, the sham of juggling different families simultaneously? What dark secrets lay hidden beneath his sickening schemes? The questions raced through my mind, their answers nonexistent, leaving me on the precipice of a frightening revelation. My head hurt with so much thinking, but I clung to the hope offered by Lola, my trusted friend. Her companionship and love meant the world to me.

"He was a killer. How could I have ever loved such a monstrous man?" The words escaped my lips, a frantic murmur in the confines of my anguish. Wearied from the ceaseless torment of my thoughts, I longed to vocalise my pain, to shatter the silence that held me captive. With each passing moment, I lay there, trapped in the clutches of despair, seeking solace and distraction. And so, I fixated on the replica painting of Mona Lisa hung on the wall opposite my bed. I stared at the woman most people in the art world believed to be *Lisa Gherardini*, the wife of a Florentine merchant. Lisa's subtle, puzzling smile, hair that fell neatly on her shoulder. Everything about her, the cryptic smile and the secrets that danced in her eyes fascinated me. She, like Ashley, remained a mystery—a riddle I had failed to unravel. Self-pity swelled within me, mingling with the bitter realisation of my foolishness.

A faint knock at the door was a welcome relief, and Lola entered, her eyes filled with a profound fondness that melted the fragile barriers I'd constructed. I was overwhelmed with gratitude, and tears streamed down my face uncontrollably. I was grateful she had stood by my side through it all.

"I came to check on you. Please tell me you're still not consumed by thoughts of Ashley," she said, her voice laced with genuine concern.

"I can't stop thinking about him," I said dully.

Lola stared at me in disbelief, her expressive face showing her concern. She had always worn her emotions openly, even in the darkest times.

"After everything he did to you? He could have condemned you to a life behind bars or, even worse—take your life. Thank God your phone captured his confession, and Chad received the right sentence for his role in Sadie's murder." Lola's eyes narrowed, her concern evident. There was a short pause, and then she added, "I don't understand how you can't despise him."

But I had no answer and couldn't respond. A profound sadness settled over me as I redirected my thoughts to the maze of unanswered questions that haunted my existence. Every word Ashley had ever spoken, every tender moment we'd shared, his profess of love until the end, was now tainted by the realisation that they were mere illusions. Our romance is a carefully crafted sham. And I, a willing participant in my own deception, oblivious to the sinister truth that lay veiled before my eyes. How could I hate a man I once loved so deeply despite the monstrous depths he had sunk to?

"You would have stayed married to him," Lola remarked, shaking her head in disbelief. Lola's face revealed her confusion; she stared at me, and I met her gaze, knowing that what I was about to say would defy reason, yet compelled to tell her my next line of action.

"My goal is to uncover the truth about Ashley's other wives and their children. Shiloh ShearJashub must know his siblings, who are dispersed across the nation. They are also his family."

Lola stood there, stunned into silence. "Why would you want to unearth the secrets of Ashley's twisted world? He was practically a stranger to you. Do you understand the danger you would be exposing yourself and Shiloh to? Don't jeopardise your son's life!"

I had no immediate response to her reproving words, but deep within me, I knew that Shiloh, when he grew older, would never forgive me if I allowed the mysteries of his father's life to remain buried. Closure eluded me, and I couldn't feign satisfaction by pretending that Ashley's death had severed all ties to his dark secrets. Death had removed the veil from my eyes, but I could no longer ignore the insatiable need for answers.

I paused, my mind racing with possibilities, uncertainties, and a burning desire for closure. "I know it sounds unbelievable, Lola, but I can't shake this feeling that there was more to the story. More to Ashley than we know, and I can't just let his secrets be buried with him. Shiloh deserves the truth, and I need to find it, no matter the cost."

Lola's eyes softened with understanding, but she still looked worried. "Christine, I can't pretend to know the depths of your pain and the need for closure, but please promise me you'll be careful. If there's one thing I've learned from this nightmare, it's that darkness lurks where we least expect it."

I nodded, determined to be careful. "I promise, Lola. I'll seek the truth, but I'll be cautious. For Shiloh's sake and mine."

She sighed, resignation evident in her voice. "Alright, Christine. But promise me you won't undertake this journey alone. We'll face whatever lies ahead together, just like we always have."

A small smile played at the corners of my lips, grateful for her support. "Thanks, Lola. I couldn't do this without you. Together, we'll uncover the truth and end this nightmare."

As I said those words, a newfound purpose coursed through my veins, and the mystery of Ashley White and his lies became a challenge I was willing to embrace. The path ahead would be dangerous but driven by a fierce resolve. I was ready to confront the darkness that awaited and uncover the truth that would set me free.

"Who was Ashley White?" I whispered with a frown, excited and cautious at the same time. The question echoed in the room as Lola stared at me, her eyes speaking words she dared not utter. I knew Lola still had doubts, but she always supported my decisions, even if marred with dangers.

***

The following day, I awoke from a fitful night's sleep, my body tangled in the bedsheets as my mind wrestled with the events of the funeral. The revelation that Ashley was a serial bigamist had left me reeling. Questions and doubts spun in my mind like dark clouds, tormenting me with their relentless presence. Seeking relief from the pounding headache and the sharp pain in my chest, I fumbled through the bedside drawer. With a sigh of relief, I found an aspirin and hastily swallowed it, washing it down with water Lola had thoughtfully placed on the bedside table. The gesture was a small comfort, and I was grateful. I collapsed on the bed, contemplating my future as Lola and Shiloh's voices drifted to my room. Lola had been staying with us for almost a month, and I dread when she has to return to her own family.

Ashley's true nature now loomed over me, haunting my thoughts like a sinister spectre. What kind of man had he been? And what kind of people had he surrounded himself with? I couldn't escape the feeling of foolishness for falling for his charms, believing his every word and gesture. But now, I had to confront the harsh truth that he was a fraud.

My brother Henry had always been sceptical of Ashley, and his doubts seemed justified. Lola, although silent, held the truth in her eyes. The time had come to shed my fears and embrace my newfound determination. I needed to unravel the mysteries of Ashley's past, to uncover the truth about his extended family in South Africa and the siblings he rarely spoke of. His Danish and Zulu ancestry painted a picture of a complex upbringing shrouded in secrecy. He always told me we have a whole lifetime to know each other. What an irony.

Lola was still sceptical, even if she said nothing. I saw the truth in her eyes but couldn't leave things as they were and not exhume the past. I was now a different woman, determined and no longer afraid of what I may unearth. I needed to know the truth about Ashley's extended family background. Does he have siblings in South Africa?

My mind still raced with thoughts of Ashley's secret life. I couldn't shake the feeling that there was more to the story than I'd been told. I knew I needed answers and closure. I couldn't and wouldn't let his secret life go unresolved. I knew it wouldn't be easy, but I had to learn more about Ashley's other wives and children. I couldn't leave Shiloh with unanswered questions about his father's past because he deserved to know the truth, no matter how hard. The poor boy almost witnessed my murder, so I don't think anything else would surprise him.

I needed to know more about Ashley's legal affairs and the extent of his deception. I had to find out how he had managed to keep so many secrets for so long. I started my investigation by contacting our family lawyer, Alistair Chaplain, who knew his sordid secrets.

Alistair agreed to meet and provide any information he could.

That evening, he came to my house looking more relaxed and less scary. I'd prepared a sumptuous dinner, and as we ate, I prodded him for more details. Surprisingly, Alistair gave me the names and addresses of the other wives. I was shocked to learn that one of them lived in Nashville. I'd imagined they may be in the States, further away from me. He declined to answer any questions about Ashley's parents and family in South Africa. As a lawyer, Alistair should know that bigamy is a criminal offence and carries at least a five-year jail term and a five hundred dollars' fine. So why was he complicit in Ashley's numerous marriages? When I asked the reason he was part of the deceptions. Alistair was visibly upset and explained that his job was not to lecture his clients but to advise them, and it was up to them to take the advice.

"Ashley was very discreet, and he usually files for divorce before remarrying again," Alistair explained between mouthfuls. He appeared to be enjoying my famous Tikka Masala. "You were technically his legal wife, and I did warn him it would come back to haunt him."

"If I was his legal wife, he wasn't a bigamist."

Alistair rolled his eyes and gave me a look that said, "You're *stupid.*"

"His divorce with his British wife was not finalised before you got hooked on him," he explained with the patience of a nursery teacher explaining how the play-dough worked for a four-year-old. We made small talk about the weather and what I would do if I found Ashley's liaisons.

Alistair's explanations were half-hearted, and I wasn't satisfied, but he was about to leave, and I was getting desperate and pressed him for additional information.

"What about his family in South Africa?"

"You would have to ask Henry," he said as I walked him to his car, his gnarled hands shaking as he wanted to open his car door.

"Henry," I asked incredulously, "my brother?"

"Yes," Alistair nodded and entered his Sedan, "Thanks for the food."

I knew I had to tread carefully while exploring this rabbit hole. I didn't want to put myself or Shiloh in danger by digging too deep. But what could Henry possibly know about Ashley? I had to confront the truth because ignoring it was no longer an option. I had to face it head-on.

PART FOUR

THE ENCOUNTER

The next morning, I contacted Jane, one of Ashley's former wives, in Nashville. We agreed to meet during the upcoming weekend, and with a newfound determination, I set my sights on driving to Nashville. As I dropped Shiloh at Lola's place, her silence spoke volumes, but her tight embrace comforted me. Like a woman possessed, I hit the road, driven by an unwavering mission. Halloween weekend awaited, and I'd secured a reservation at the Armitage Hotel, where I would meet with Jane in the lobby.

My journey to Nashville was uneventful.

I was pleased when the valet took charge of parking my car on arrival. Walking towards the grand doors of the Armitage Hotel, my heart raced with anticipation. As I entered the lobby, the luxurious surroundings pulled me in, and I loved what I saw. The hotel walls were decorated with dark wood panelling, while the marble floors gleamed in a luminous mix of gold and cream. The warm glow of crystal chandeliers suspended from the ceiling enhanced the atmosphere. Luxurious armchairs and sofas, draped in silky shades of deep red and gold, enticed guests to sink into them. My fatigue made me want to collapse into the armchair. But I remembered the reason I was at the hotel. This wasn't a luxurious break. I came for serious business. My eyes caught the delicate crystal glasses and silver bowls filled with vibrant floral arrangements adorned elegant side tables, infusing the air with a refreshing scent. A grand piano highlighted the hotel's elegance with a glossy black finish that reflected the shimmering light in a corner. The front lobby had a sweeping staircase that ascended to the second floor, complete with a carved ornate bannister. A historical battle scene depicted in a striking painting above the stairs captured everyone's attention.

The reception desk, crafted from polished marble, catered to a queue of well-dressed guests awaiting their turn to check-in. As I approached the smiling reception staff, my heartbeat increased, and I clasped my bag tightly to diffuse my rising tension.

Don't panic, everything will work out fine, I thought and forced a smile on my face, rejecting the anxiety threatening to engulf me. I stood in line and looked around, allowing my mind to dwell on my surroundings. My eyes were drawn to the captivating painting above the fireplace, and I wondered who the artist was. I made a mental note to ask the hotel staff before checking out.

I noticed the subtle fragrance in the air courtesy of a large vase filled with fresh Iris flowers, adding a touch of tranquillity to the space. *I'll get the flower tomorrow,* I thought, as my eyes roved around for the last time. The hotel had an undeniable charm, but my palms were sweaty because of my nervousness, which was understandable because of my impending meeting. I completed the check-in process, receiving my room card without fully registering the details. I left the lobby and approached the elevator. I almost bumped into a group of teenagers laughing with no care in the world. I envied their problem-free lives. I ambled to the elevator, came out, and strolled to my hotel room. I feared it would become a battleground for my emotions.

With an hour left before my scheduled meeting with Jane, I rummaged through my handbag, retrieving my phone with weary hands. The impulse to reach out to Lola was strong, but something held me back. Collapsing onto the bed, I caught sight of my reflection in the mirror—an image that has borne the brunt of the past few weeks. Endowed with natural beauty, the green eyes that once sparkled with life, an average height that exuded confidence, pale white skin reminiscent of moonlight, long blonde hair cascading down my back, and an hourglass figure that had turned heads in the past seemed like a mirage. I looked like a shadow of my former self. Neglect had etched its mark upon me, leaving behind dark circles beneath my eyes, a dullness that marred my flawless skin, and hair that had lost its lustre, resembling a tangled mess. The exhaustion in my eyes was a testament to the toll that Ashley's tragic end had taken on my spirit. At that moment, I mirrored Lola's dishevelled state when she first discovered the heart-wrenching truth of Sadie's murder.

I lay motionless on the bed, my body frozen, as my breath echoed in the room. Each inhale and exhale reverberated, a constant reminder of the tension coursing through my veins. Thoughts raced through my mind like sprinters in a relay race, gunning for a prize and, in my case, a desperate attempt to plan the words I would speak to Jane. The upcoming meeting filled me with a deep dread, yet I knew I had no choice but to face it head-on. Now alone, I wasn't as brave as I thought.

It felt like I had stumbled upon a hidden truth, a dark secret lurking beneath the surface. The thought of meeting with Jane reminded me of a film I watched years ago about a couple who booked an innocent-looking Airbnb room, only to discover too late that the hosts were malicious serial killers. What *if* Jane was an evil, desperate woman seeking revenge? What *if* she blamed me for breaking up her marriage and making her children fatherless? The 'what-ifs' swirled through my mind as realisation struck me with chilling intensity, sending shivers down my spine. It was as if fate had sealed my destiny, binding me to this challenging encounter without offering a single escape route. *But it wasn't fate,* I mused; *it was me. I set up the whole meeting.*

As the worst-case scenario played out in my mind, I knew it was my fear creating chaos in my head. I smiled, and it gave me a break from the constant worry. I was aware of and noticed the irony in my thoughts. Whenever I faced uncertainty, my mind always came up with strange things that might happen, drawing parallels between my situation and a terrifying scenario. I truly put my imagination to the test, proving that even in the bleakest moments, I conjured up intricate stories that had no connection to reality. I expressed my frustration by gritting my teeth and letting out a loud grunt.

I glanced at my wristwatch, anxious and frightened, each passing second feeling like an eternity. I hated waiting because I was not a patient person. Time dragged on with excruciating slowness, intensifying the weight of anticipation in the air, dragging its feet as if to mock my impatience. The tension bore down on me, heightening the suspense in the air like a heavy fog.

I sought relief from my restless mind and found myself wandering to a secluded chamber where memories of my father were stored. But as I explored my mind further, I discovered a disturbing void - a part of me that I had hidden away and seldom visited.

Dad had always been closer to Henry, his attention reserved for my older brother. In contrast, he treated me with an unsettling fragility, as if I were a delicate flower on the verge of wilting at any moment, and I hated it. This peculiar dynamic between us was a source of constant conflict between my parents. Their rows revolved around the perceived favouritism and their differing perspectives on how to handle me. The weight of their battles pressed upon my heart, and I was caught in the crossfire of their fractured love. I sighed. Their constant bickering shaped my existence and cast a shadow over my identity.

Even when I was wrong, my mum stood up for me. I perceived she was guarding me against unforeseen risks, or maybe she recognised herself in me. She never talked about her parents. My life has been a never-ending cycle of secrets, from my parents and grandparents to my deceased husband. What a life!

The clock's ticking continued its relentless march, echoing in the room, a sad reminder of the passing moments. My weary mind won, and I slept, hanging between reality and the languid, floaty feeling of dreaming. And then, at last, my alarm sounded. It was time. I took a deep breath, a mix of relief and apprehension. But before leaving the room, I locked away my complicated feelings about my father again. It was a temporary measure, a self-imposed mechanism to shield myself from emotional turmoil.

But a realisation dawned upon me as I sealed the door to those unresolved emotions. It was time to confront the ghosts of my past and see a therapist to untangle my complex upbringing. Seeking professional help had been at the back of my mind. Lola had encouraged me to see a therapist, but I'd always brushed it off. I hated the idea of telling a stranger my deep-seated secrets. But she'd argue it would be therapeutic, that seeing a psychiatrist would ease my mental anguish. As usual, Lola was right. I made a mental note to arrange a meeting, acknowledging the pressing need to dissect my history and find solace in sharing my burdens.

Mustering every ounce of determination, I rose from the bed, a renewed resolve driving me. With a flourish, I opened the door, closed it behind me and went down the long hallway to the lift. Jane should be in the lobby now.

But she wasn't, so I sat and waited for fifteen minutes. And then I saw her. She stood tall at the hotel entrance, scanning everyone, looking for me. She looked posh and beautiful, and I felt self-conscious about my frazzled appearance. I forced a smile onto my face and waved my hands, beckoning to her.

Jane saw me and her eyes lit up as she moved towards my table. I watched her approach in admiration. Her long, dark hair cascaded luxuriously over her shoulders, and her high cheekbones accentuated her sharp features, lending an air of regal sophistication to her already striking appearance. She wore a tailored navy pantsuit that hugged her curves, and she looked confident from afar. She was a gorgeous woman, and I felt a slight tinge of envy, but the seriousness of the situation facing me was mammoth. I pushed vain thoughts away.

I watched as Jane approached and noticed her eyes. They were like pools of deep waters and throbbing with pain. It showed she was battling with sorrow that ran deep. I guessed the revelation of Ashley's death and the existence of several wives and children would have shattered the illusion of a seemingly perfect marriage for Jane.

At least, that was how I felt.

I stood up with a genuine smile. We hugged briefly, and I caught a whiff of Jane's perfume, *Caligna by Dora Baghriche*, one of my favourite fragrances; the scent sent me straight to the South of France. I motioned Jane to a seat opposite mine. A waiter came, and we ordered red wine. As we waited for our orders, our eyes locked, and the room seemed silent, as if we were the only occupants in the lobby already brimming with the hubbub of voices and soft jazz music playing to assuage frayed nerves. Jane's dark brown eyes betrayed a hint of exhaustion. Beneath her stoic exterior, I sensed a stormy sea of emotions raging to spill out, a combination of grief, anger, and confusion. I've been there and could empathise.

Jane nervously adjusted the delicate diamond pendant hanging from her neck, and her fingers trembled as they brushed against the cool metal. We made eye contact, and I felt both grateful and suspicious that she had agreed to meet me. Our conversation was overshadowed by our shared experiences, leaving uncertainty between us. I smiled and spoke clearly, despite the inner turmoil I felt.

"What a lovely pendant you have. Was it a gift?"

"Yes," Jane answered quietly, looking at me coolly. "Ashley gave it to me on our tenth anniversary.

The revelation felt like a knife stabbing my heart and soul, causing me to gasp. The woman seated opposite me was Ashley's partner for a decade! We were married for the same duration. *Alistair conveniently forgot to mention that. I think he lied to me!* I swallowed hard, masking my emotions, but before I spoke, the waiter arrived with our wine, and I gulped it down quickly, trying to regain my composure.

Across from each other, we engaged in a wordless battle of suspicion and curiosity. I watched Jane with a mix of caution and curiosity. We were both afraid, yet we shared a common goal of unravelling the intricacies of our husband's double life.

Jane's voice trembled as she spoke, her eyes glistening with tears, and I noticed her trembling lips. Her tone measured.

"How long have you known about … about us?"

I met her stare with understanding in my eyes. "Not long," I admitted, my voice tinged with sadness and resignation. "I discovered his betrayal after his passing, hidden in the depths of his meticulously kept records." I didn't want to reveal the complete truth or mention Alistair until I knew Jane could be trusted.

Surprise crossed Jane's face. I imagined the revelation that her late husband had deceived us both was a bitter pill to swallow. We fell into companionable silence, alone with our troubled thoughts. I wondered if she would want to visit Ashley's grave, but decided it was up to her. If she wished to, I wouldn't mind taking her.

Moments later, I leaned towards her, my voice cautious yet filled with intrigue. My curiosity was piqued.

"Jane, tell me more about how your relationship with Ashley began. How did you two meet?"

For a moment, Jane paused while different expressions crossed her face. The memories flooding her mind may have been from their first encounter.

"It was like something out of a romance novel, Christine. I'd just returned from a trip to Kenya, exhausted but exhilarated. As I waited at the John F. Kennedy Airport carousel in New York to reclaim my luggage, our eyes met across the bustling crowd. There was an instant connection, an undeniable spark."

I arched my eyebrows at the revelation. The unfolding story captivated me. I pressed for more information.

"And who would have thought that meeting would lead to marriage? What drew you to Ashley?"

Jane's lips curled into a nostalgic smile, a mixture of fondness and sadness.

"He was charming and intelligent, Christine. Ashley was pursuing his doctorate while I was a lecturer at Harvard. We bonded over our shared passion for academia and the world of ideas. The conversations were electric, and before I knew it, we were inseparable. Two months later, we were married."

I leaned in closer, yearning for every detail of their romance. It was hard to imagine that the man we talked about was also my husband, but I was caught up in the moment.

"Two months of dating, and you were married. That's quite the leap. How did it all happen?" I remarked with a pang of guilt. I married Ashley after a mere twelve weeks, but I was not ready to divulge those details yet.

Jane's gaze shifted, a flicker of vulnerability crossing her face.

"It felt right," she whispered as if someone might be eavesdropping. "We couldn't think of a life without each other, or at least that was what I believed. Our vows marked the beginning of a journey I thought would be full of love and happiness. During my sabbatical, we travelled worldwide, immersing ourselves in various cultures. After two years, we were blessed with twin sons, Jonathan and Peter. I had the impression that our family was complete. I was completely mistaken."

The burden of the past hung heavily in the air, suffocating us. I could feel Jane's agony seeping into my bones, and I squeezed her hands, desperate to convey my empathy. Our eyes locked, as if searching for solace in each other's souls. And then, in a calm tone, I spoke.

"It's twisted, isn't it, Jane? To have known a love so deep, only to have it shattered by the lies that lay hidden beneath. I can't even fathom the rollercoaster of emotions you must have endured. I'm still grappling with my pain, which is why I reached out to you, why I needed to meet."

A fleeting smile flitted across Jane's face, but it was brief, overshadowed by the torment etched into every word that flowed from her lips. Her voice trembled, carrying the stress of her past in every syllable that escaped her lips.

"The realisation has been devastating. To discover that the man I believed I knew was a master of deception, hiding a web of lies that entangled other wives and children. The betrayal cuts to the core of my being, but I am resolved to face the truth—for my sake and my sons."

I held onto her hands, our bond solidifying with each passing second, and for the first time that day, a genuine smile graced Jane's lips, reaching her eyes with a shimmer of hope, piercing through the pain.

"We're in this together, Jane," I reassured her warmly, returning her smile with an understanding nod. "We'll uncover the truth and bring justice to light. No matter how dark it gets, we'll support each other, drawing strength from our shared experiences."

Jane nodded, her spirit rekindling with a renewed sense of determination. The weight of our burdens seemed to lessen as we acknowledged our intertwined fates.

"Thank you, Christine, for reaching out," Jane whispered, gratitude resonating in her words. "Most women would shy away from knowing the other woman. But together, we'll piece the fragment of Ashley's lies and find the closure we deserve. Our paths have converged for a reason, and we won't allow his deceit to define us."

At that moment, our meeting took on a new dimension. It transformed into a partnership forged in the ruins of broken trust, a union born from our shared pain. The initial wariness thawed, replaced by a begrudging sense of camaraderie. Without uttering a word, we understood each other, bound by the knowledge of the deep wounds inflicted by the deceit that had brought us together. It was a collision of shattered dreams and broken trust, an encounter that would forever alter the trajectory of our lives. We shared stories of missed red flags and whispered anecdotes that hinted at the extent of the deception we had endured. Emotions churned within us—hurt, anger, and an overwhelming need for closure.

As the evening wore on, we became more comfortable around each other, and we chatted easily, swapping stories about Ashley's work trips and the times he was probably visiting his other families. We had a fragile connection, and we both felt it. Jane reached out and held my hands with a shy smile on her face. I returned her smile, thinking of the pain she must have gone through. We both found solace in each other's presence, knowing that we were not alone in our difficult situation. An alliance began to form tentatively, pushed by our shared determination to unearth the truth despite lingering suspicion.

"Yes, we won't," I agreed with her earlier statement, and then a thought struck me. "Do you have any of Ashley's family photos? Or perhaps pictures of him? It will help us piece together the puzzle."

Jane took out her phone and showed me a series of pictures. Ashley's rugged smile beamed from the screen. But something felt strange. I had never seen him like this before; his usually intense and piercing brown eyes had turned a shade of grey, and his entire demeanour had softened, showing a gentle, almost mellow expression. Was Ashley using coloured contact lenses? As I swiped to the next image, I couldn't help but gasp.

The twins. They were the spitting image of Shiloh, with their thick mop of brown hair, cheeky smiles, and olive-brown skin.

"How old are your children?" I asked, even though deep down, I already knew the answer. Ashley was still married to Jane when we first met. *Alistair conveniently forgot to mention that detail.* Jane's eyes lit up, and love radiated from her beautiful face.

"They will turn ten on the 8th of December," she replied, her voice filled with warmth.

I froze, the air around us growing still. My son Shiloh shared the same birth date, day, month, and year. How could this be? Jane caught the distress in my expression, her eyes wide with disbelief and fear. Wordlessly, she implored me to explain.

"I have an only son, Shiloh..." My voice trailed off, realisation crushing my words.

"Our children were born on the same day, the same month, the same year?" Jane whispered, her voice barely audible, dripping with fear.

I nodded, unable to find words to explain the truth that loomed over us. There was no need for further explanation. I was afraid and felt a tightening in my throat. I gritted my teeth in frustration as our shared pain expanded, morphing into something even more sinister. Whatever we were dealing with had just grown larger, and the presence of a mystery beyond comprehension was before us, waiting to be solved.

PART FIVE

THE GHOST

As the black cab cruised through the rain-drenched city of London, the deep, throaty voices of Gregorian chants' *Asperges Me Domine* coursed into my body through my earpiece; the only words I know of Latin, *Glory be to the Father and the to Son and to the Holy Ghost.* The unforgiving weather pummelled the cab as large droplets of rain pounded my taxi, and the sound intermingled with the turmoil in my heart. The rest of the song soothed my frayed nerves as my search for truth took me to England.

Lola was more than happy to take care of Shiloh for a week. Her daughter, Melody, five years old, was besotted with my son. I couldn't help but daydream about a future where Shiloh and Melody would grow up together and perhaps even marry someday. I was one of the people who hated arranged marriages, and to think I could be at the

forefront of it was because of my experience. I now understand why parents are keen to know everything about their
children's partners before they marry them. It was a fleeting thought, born out of a desire for a sense of stability and
belonging in this complex journey I had embarked upon. A
sigh escaped me as I wondered if I was doing the right
thing. My over-analytic brain was tired of looking for pot-
holes and pitfalls. I was usually optimistic, but now, I see
problems in everything and suspect everyone of having
hidden agendas.

As I was lost in thought, my phone chimed, notifying
me of a text message.

***I am thinking of you. I hope everything goes well to-
day – J.***

A bittersweet smile crossed my face as I replied with a
smiley face and prayer emoji. Jane's message warmed my
heart, but the sadness that accompanied it reminded me of
the risks I was taking and the toll on me.

The weight of my mission and the increasing connec-
tions in my life overwhelmed me. My search for the truth
about Ashley's past and his marriages led me to Jane, who
had become an important part of my life. The revelation
that our children had the same birthday was a peculiar coincidence that both intrigued and disturbed us.

It's strange how I accepted Jane and her children into
my life, and there I was, thinking I was alone with only
Shiloh and Lola. My familial ties have now expanded.

Looking for a dead husband's wife was one of the craziest things any woman could do, but I was restless. I would not rest until I uncovered his true identity and discovered the mysterious story behind Ashley White.

Jane and I agreed to stay in touch and nurture our friendship, even making plans to celebrate Christmas together. But Lola, cautious by nature and, because of her profession as a lawyer, complained about my relationship with Jane and her children, warning me about potential dangers. Frustrated, I reminded her that Jane and I were married to the same man for a decade, emphasising the bond we now shared. Whether I liked, it was irrelevant because Jane's twin sons are now Shiloh's step-brothers. I knew Lola was worried about me and Shiloh, but when she saw I was determined about it, she dropped the subject. Although her apprehensive eyes betrayed her lingering doubts. Her intuitive nature served her well in her career, but I questioned its relevance in my personal life.

I was determined to unearth my late husband's mysterious identity and knew I couldn't let doubts or caution hold me back. This was my life, and I was willing to take risks and face the unknown in my quest for answers. The secrets and lies surrounding Ashley White needed to be exposed, and I was determined to do so, no matter the cost.

The cab crawled to a stop in front of a stately, sprawling Romanesque mansion in St John's Wood as the rain bombarded us mercilessly. I marvelled at the towering round arches and stone brick walls, but the downpour left me disoriented. The rain fell like bombs on a raiding mission. It brought to mind London during the Blitz, and I couldn't help but wonder what it must have been like living in the city during those intense bombing raids in World War Two. Shaking my head at the absurd comparison of rain to falling bombs, I acknowledged that my thoughts were chaotic. *How could I compare rain to falling bombs?* What Lola said was true. I have an atypical mind. I allowed my thoughts to play around the rain, and as I studied the pooling water on the car window, each drop seemed to outdo the other as if competing for attention. In a moment of whimsy, I imagined the raindrops as jealous lovers hellbent on wreaking havoc on an ex, relentless and unforgiving. I jokingly named the rain 'home wrecker,' amused by my peculiar mind. It was persistent and unforgiving, and the rain hemmed us in.

Uncertain whether to leave the cab, the affable Bangladeshi driver turned to me with the broadest smile I'd ever seen. "Madam, you can wait for a while until the rain subsides. It's no problem, and I won't charge you extra," he kindly offered. And he smiled again. His face reminded me of a wrinkled orange I saw on my last trip to Ethiopia.

"Thank you," I said with a grateful smile, unsure if I would accept his offer. The heavens seemed to agree with him as the torrents intensified. I sank back into the seat, mentally preparing the questions I would ask Florence. My confidence had grown after the meeting with Jane, and I was determined to wrap up everything in London before Thanksgiving and return home.

A sickening thought dampened my optimism because I also had to see Henry and dreaded it. With a quick sigh, I pushed thoughts of Henry's thoughts aside and focused on the task at hand. Double-checking the address Florence gave me, I was amazed at her opulence. As the rain blanketed us, I peered at the imposing building and loved what I saw. The leafy, quiet street of St. John's Wood was a stark contrast to the bustling London I had anticipated. I quickly Googled the area and discovered many ex-pats, especially Americans, lived there.

Finally, 'home wrecker' lost momentum and settled into a shower I could manage. I thanked the kind cab driver and stepped out onto the cobblestone street of St. John's Wood. Surprisingly, I was feeling cold. I thought I was prepared for London weather but felt a chill as the rain and breeze assaulted my beige sweater, blue jeans, and nude knee-length boots. I wished I'd brought a thicker jacket with a hood as I rushed towards the imposing black gate and pressed the intercom.

As the gate flung open and I made my way up the winding driveway, I couldn't help but feel like an outsider, a stranger in a world that was not my own. I was thrust into this investigative journey thanks to Ashley's sordid past.

When I reached the front door, Florence, who was every bit the aristocratic lady I had expected her to be, greeted me warmly. She was tall and regal, with perfect posture and a commanding presence. Her blonde hair was perfectly coiffed, and her piercing blue eyes seemed to take in everything around her with a sharpness that made me feel exposed. I realised Ashley had a penchant for tall, beautiful women, and it seemed rather strange that he ended up with me as his last wife because I was anything but tall. It was odd, to say the least. I know I am beautiful in my own right, but Jane and Florence were in a class of their own - stylish, sophisticated and elegant.

I continued down the long hallway, my chunky boots pounding against the marble floors, as Florence led me to a grand sitting room in her sprawling mansion. A short smile played around the corner of my mouth as I recalled Lola's praise of my beauty.

"Your piercing green eyes are like the eyes of an angel, and you have this look of a kind woman, Christine. You are a lovely woman."

"Thanks, Lola!" I said in appreciation and roared into laughter.

I don't think I was in the same class as the woman staring at me as if she wanted to extract secrets from my soul. As we sat to tea in the grand drawing room, Florence began opening up about her life with Ashley. She spoke of their travels together and the lavish gifts she gave him. But her voice had an underlying tension, hinting at something she wasn't revealing.

The conversation eventually turned to the sprawling house. I watched Florence, intrigued, as she told me the villa's history, of how it had been passed down through her family for generations. She pointed out the intricate details of the elaborate furnishings, from the chandeliers that hung from the ceiling to the vintage rugs that lined the floor.

But even as I admired the house, I couldn't shake off the feeling that something was wrong. I felt secrets lurking beneath the surface, waiting to be uncovered. I decided on the same tactics I used for Jane and asked direct questions. I hadn't flown from Huntsville to admire the mansion, no matter how beautiful. But I sensed that Florence would be a thicker nut to crack; she was way much older, and I wondered if that would be a disadvantage to me.

"So, how did you meet Ashley, Florence?" I asked sounding friendly.

Florence took a sip of her tea, then put down her cup. "I met him at a charity event in Mayfair. He was charming, and we clicked instantly," she replied with a smile.

I mulled that over. *A charity event at Mayfair?* That doesn't say much. Intrigued, I prodded for more information.

"How long ago was that, if I may ask?"

"That was thirty-five years ago," she answered, looking at me shrewdly. She was watching my reaction, and I sensed Florence was enjoying this. She was like a detective, watching a criminal's every move. I shifted on my seat, trying to steer the conversation to safer grounds.

"That's interesting," I said, and something clicked in my brain. I was three years old when they met. Florence could be pushing towards sixty, and I felt my skin crawl. I studied her smooth, wrinkleless face and concluded she must be using Botox. Frustrated with my straying thoughts, I wheeled my mind back to the present.

"How can that be?" I asked, the surprise evident in my voice.

"He was a kid when we met, ten years old," she explained with a chuckle, a mischievous glint in her eyes. "I was much older. I was twenty and married with a husband fond of phantom business trips. Ashley had maturity beyond his years. His adoptive parents lived quite close to us, and his interest in the Arts endeared me to him. We became friends, and he looked up to me. It was years before we fell in love."

I allowed that to sink in, and as we continued talking, I heard a voice that made me panic, and my hair stood on end.

"Anybody home?"

The voice was familiar, unmistakably Ashley's. But that couldn't be. He died right in front of me. I organised his funeral after an autopsy confirmed his death. My heart raced as I turned to see the impossible - Ashley, standing there, looking younger and full of life. Stunned and disoriented, I felt a rush of dizziness. I stared at the tall, muscular man in disbelief as he strolled into the drawing room. His hair was the same, and his bright brown eyes twinkled with mischief. For some strange reason, my eyes went straight to his hands and then to the proximal wrist crease, and I noticed three stars that looked like birthmarks. Ashley had the same birthmark, and Shiloh had only a one-star birthmark since birth. Every doctor who ever examined him always commented on the strange birthmark.

My heartbeat increased as our eyes locked. He looked fresh, tan and as handsome as ever. We stared at each other, and that same spell of dizziness again, and I held the chair for support. That moment when he had the gun to his head replayed in my mind, and my mouth felt dry. *No, it can't be. This must be Ashley's ghost.* My thoughts were frantic, and if I wasn't careful, I might have a heart attack, which was the last thing I remembered.

***

I came around to see Ashley's *ghost* staring at me, and I heard the fear in his voice,

"Do you think she's alright, mum?"

"She will be," I heard Florence drawl, unperturbed.

Mum? My confusion grew as four pairs of eyes burrowed into mine. Florence's stony visage showed neither concern nor fear, making me wonder if fainting spells were common in her home. I felt an urge to leave, but I needed answers. The *ghost* handed me a cup of water, which I drank to regain my composure. I turned my questioning glance to Florence, determined to discover the truth.

"He's your son?" I asked in a hoarse voice, still wrapping my head around the situation and wondering for the umpteenth time the story behind the man scrutinising me, the same way an Egyptologist would study mummified remains. Ignoring my question, Florence turned her attention to the *ghost*. They exchanged glances, and I sensed his reluctance, and then he nodded and disappeared into one of the many rooms in the house. I felt uneasy, unsure if coming to see Florence was the right decision. My fainting spells had started recently, possibly due to stress, but now I questioned if I needed professional help. It started shortly after my trip to Nashville. If I'd told Lola about it, she would've discouraged me from visiting London.

Florence turned to me and smiled, but it didn't reach her cold blue eyes.

"Yes, he's my son, and his name is Angel. That's not Ashley." Florence confirmed, dropping a bombshell that left me both relieved and disappointed. I realised I needed a clear mind to unravel the threads of Ashley's past, and Florence seemed to hold crucial information about him that Alistair and my brother didn't know.

Feeling overwhelmed, I closed my eyes and allowed that to sink in. I knew I couldn't trust my judgment until I sorted out the facts. The mysteries surrounding Ashley's life drove me to the edge, and I needed to regain control of the situation. Visiting a psychiatrist seemed like a wise decision to ensure my mental clarity as I probed deeper into Ashley's complicated history. But when that would happen, it remained hazy. Probably after the New Year, I'll sort something out.

"Ashley and I got together when he turned twenty-one, eleven years later. By that time, I'd divorced my husband," Florence began, a sad expression on her face. I listened attentively, poking holes in her story and wondering if she was telling me the truth. It wasn't easy to know who to trust again. I focused my attention on her voice, trying to capture every detail.

"We raised many eyebrows because of our age difference, but who cares!" Her emotions exploded, and I was caught off guard by her contorted face. She paused, then continued. "We got married, and Ashley moved in with me. But the problem started after Angel's birth. Ashley's obsession with finding his birth parents took him to Durban in South Africa. By then, his adoptive parents had died in a strange arson attack. Their house burnt to the ground." Florence stopped speaking as if thinking about her next words.

"I need to be honest with you," Florence continued, her voice quivering with anxiety. "I feared Ashley. After his trip to Durban, he returned a changed man, and the darkness in him was real. It was as if a different man or something or someone had taken over him. I thought it was the grief over his adoptive parents, but there was something else, something sinister. He started associating with these men in black robes, and they seemed to have a strange influence on him. He also started drinking, but those men ... they had a hold on him."

She stopped speaking because Angel was back in the drawing room. Florence motioned him to a chair, and he sat down, avoiding eye contact with me. I sat across from Florence, her words echoing as I maintained a calm composure. Inside, my heart pounded with excitement and fear. The revelations she had shared were like pieces of a puzzle falling into place, but the picture they were forming was chilling. Florence had hired a private detective to investigate the dark secrets surrounding Ashley's past, and what she uncovered was beyond her wildest imagination.

"Ashley was not a single child," she said, her eyes sparkling. "He was part of a set of triplets. Also, there's a sinister organisation called 'The Sons of Nephilim' that's been after children like Ashley for centuries. Because dark secrets surrounded their births, 'The Sons of Nephilim' are desperate to keep them hidden or dead."

She paused for a while and continued, "That's why I hired a private detective. I had to find out what happened to him in Durban and who these people were. And that was when we discovered the truth. I've gathered evidence that these 'Sons of Nephilim' have operated secretly for almost a thousand years. Their primary mission is to eliminate any humans who possess fallen angels' DNA, fearing the power they might wield. Ashley and his brothers are suspected of having that DNA, so they've become targets."

"The Sons of Nephilim?" I said in a low voice, and Florence nodded.

Was Ashley a triplet? That explains it. Maybe Jane was married to one of the triplets, not my Ashley. It was possible. I held my head in my hands, feeling the gravity of Florence's revelations. She appeared more comfortable with me and was keen to share more information. I've heard about the *Sons of Nephilim* from my mum. I was around 12 years old and had stumbled into her arguing with Dad in the family's library.

"These people are evil! What do you know about the Sons of Nephilim?" Mum had shouted, and when they both saw me, they screeched,

"GET OUT!" Although Mum later came to apologise, I'd already seen a darker, more furious side of her that day.

"Florence, I can't believe what you're telling me," I whispered, steadying my nerves. "This is beyond anything I've ever encountered. I came to you because Ashley killed a woman and then turned the gun on himself, and then I realised he was a bigamist. And now, you're telling me he was not a lone child but part of a triplet, and this strange occultic group is after Ashley and his brothers?"

"Yes," Florence answered.

"But how can I trust you? Why are you telling me this now?"

Florence stood up and walked to the tall window in the drawing room, her slim fingers tracing the curtains. I watched her keenly. The more I dug into Ashley's life, the more I felt a strange stirring in my heart. There was always a clue missing, and I had this nagging fear that someone, somewhere, was hiding things from me. Call it gut feelings, but I now know that Ashley wasn't the only danger lurking in the shadows, and that was a discomforting thought. Florence turned to face me, her piercing blue eyes glistening with unshed tears.

"I'm telling you because I am a mother and will protect my son with the last drop of my blood!"

The room seemed to close in around me as Florence's words filled my ears. I can settle for that. I love Shiloh more than life, and I would defend him with everything I have. I took a deep breath and exhaled.

Suddenly, a rueful grin crossed Florence's face, and I wondered if she had a bipolar personality—her mood swings from one end of the spectrum to another.

"I also had you watched," she said. "I knew everything about Ashley's wives."

That doesn't come as a shock. She had the money and the means to have people tailed.

"Right," I said.

Florence was prone to mood swings. She looked anxious, and her fear was infectious as it permeated the atmosphere and invaded my space, crawling through my skin and melting with my rapid heartbeat. My mind raced. Connecting the dots between Ashley's transformation and the mysterious organisation Florence mentioned sent shivers down my spine, and I knew this was far bigger than I could handle alone.

The gravity of the situation settled on my shoulders. Florence had taken the risk of digging into these dangerous secrets. Ashley was not only dealing with his demons but also with a dark, ancient force that sought to control or eliminate him. How in heaven's name am I going to protect Shiloh and Jane's twin sons? How do I defend myself? Why in heaven's name did my paths cross with Ashley's? The questions assailed my mind, and the answers eluded me.

However, Florence was not done with the bombshells.

"When I realised we were in danger, I confronted Ashley about the information I had about the Sons of Nephilim," Florence continued, her voice choked with emotion. "But he... he attacked me. He hated me investigating his heritage behind his back ... without telling him. He was furious, insinuating that I was a racist who never loved him. His words hurt, and I knew I had lost him. I only wanted to help." She choked back tears but pressed on with her story. "I had to escape with Angel to one of my family's remote castles in Scotland. They couldn't follow us there; that was the last time I saw Ashley."

I imagined the fear and pain she must have endured. But Florence's determination didn't waver; she was keen to find Ashley's brothers and warn them about the impending danger.

"And there's more," she said quietly. "*The Sons of Nephilim* will attempt to kill Ashley's children before their tenth birthday. Something about them reaching adulthood in their powers: that was why I had to live in hiding with Angel until after his tenth birthday. We returned when my private detectives told me about Ashley's death. I believed I owed him a duty to find his other families, and as luck would have it, you called. But now, I fear for Shiloh and Jane's children."

The realisation hit me hard, like an electric shock. My son's life was in danger, along with other innocent lives. A mission to gather information has turned into a fight for survival. I jumped out of my seat, but what Florence said next left me petrified.

"Christine, you need to ask Henry about the *Sons of Nephilim*," Florence urged, her eyes pleading. "I know it sounds strange, but he might have some information to help us. There is a connection there. At least that was what my private detective said."

Florence offered to have one of her drivers take me to Henry's house in Notting Hill, West London, but I declined. I wanted to be alone. I promised to call her about my findings, and she told me to be safe. Before I left, Angel walked over to me and gave me a tight hug. As I stared into his eyes, I felt a strange sensation crawl up my spine. It was as if I was looking at Ashley. The resemblance was too creepy.

I left Florence's house, and my mind raced with a million questions. Henry, my brother, was involved in this, too? It made little sense, but I knew I had to find answers. I kept amassing questions and a few answers. Then I remembered Alistair also told me to ask Henry about Ashley's family in Pretoria. That wasn't a coincidence. Alistair and Florence knew something they weren't telling me.

The rain had stopped, and the air smelt fresh. As I waited for my Uber driver, my thoughts were in chaos. The turmoil in my soul was palpable. I had to return to Shiloh and inform the police about Florence's findings. But would they even believe me?

Fallen angel's DNA.

It looked like the stuff of films. It makes no sense.

As my Uber driver cruised to a stop in front of Florence's palatial home, I glanced back and saw both mother and son looking out of their window, and I felt despondent. Their wealth did not exempt them from the painful realities of life. They have lived a sad and lonely life.

I reviewed everything Florence told me and found a hole in her tale. She still couldn't trace Ashley's and his brothers' biological parents. The truth may lie in their discovery, or the truth may debunk the angel DNA theories. I don't believe the complete story, but that nagging fear returned in intensity.

What if Florence and her private eye were right?

PART SIX

THE SONS OF NEPHILIM

I walked along the quiet streets of Notting Hill in London, enjoying the views and admiring the tall trees that graced the sidewalks and the opulent million-pound houses tucked behind their leafy screens. My mind wandered, imagining the hidden stories these closed doors might conceal. My Uber driver's mistake had led me to the wrong address. He agreed to reroute and take me to the right address, but I declined and insisted on walking.

I continued on foot, relishing the refreshing aroma of damp earth after heavy rain. The smell of rain lingered in the air after the heavy downpour, and the sun emerged from behind the clouds, casting a brilliant glow. A surge of anticipation lifted my spirits, knowing I would soon reunite with Shiloh and Lola in less than a day. I had rescheduled my flight based on the unsettling revelations from

Florence. I couldn't bear to be separated from my son any longer than necessary.

I reached the address where Henry, my estranged brother, lived. Nervousness mingled with curiosity as I approached the door. It had been almost ten years since I had seen Henry because of our differences and his refusal to accept Ashley as my partner. His loathing for Ashley was well justified, but his audacity never ceased to amaze me.

The door opened, revealing my brother – tall, middle-aged, with dark hair and a stern expression. He looked so much like our dad, but that was where the resemblance ended. While Dad had been affectionate and controlling, Henry had resisted his influence. We exchanged no pleasantries, just cold scrutiny from Henry's grey eyes as he assessed me. I was determined, though uneasy, as I embarked on this quest for answers.

"What do you want?" Henry's tone was cold, detached.

No hellos, no feigned familiarity. I might as well be speaking to a bank clerk. No one would have guessed we were related.

"I need to speak with you," I responded, my voice firm. "It's about Ashley. Startling revelations have come to light about him, and Alistair, our family lawyer, mentioned your name as someone who could shed light on everything. I need to dig into Ashley's family background."

Henry's icy behaviour thawed, granting me entry. "Come in," he said, leading me through a spacious hallway into the living room.

The room gave off a minimalist and sophisticated vibe, with its modern and luxurious furnishings and pristine white walls. The memories of chasing Henry during our childhood flooded back, and I felt a longing for a closer sibling bond, especially for Shiloh's sake. A positive male figure in his life was something I wanted for my son, but how do we repair the damage of a decade? How do I do it? The thoughts came in fast and I focused on one thing at a time. That would have been Mum's advice.

"What do you want to know about his background, Christine? Didn't you ask him about his family before marrying the guy?" Henry asked, pouring himself a glass of water with an almost ceremonial elegance. I declined his offer of orange juice and settled on the sofa, tensed and anxious. I knew this was my toughest test. Henry's eyes rested on mine.

"I'm looking for information about Ashley's family background," I said calmly. "I've been in contact with one of his ex-wives, Florence, who hinted that you might have some insights. Alistair, my family lawyer, also mentioned your name, and that's the reason I'm here."

Henry frowned. "I don't know what she's been telling you, but I know nothing about Ashley's family."

Sensing his evasiveness, I pondered how best to extract the truth from him. Our relationship had been strained, and Henry's guarded nature further complicated matters. A new approach was in order. Henry hated liars, and telling him the truth would garner his sympathy.

"Henry," I began, choosing my words with care, "Please, I'm asking for your help. Ashley is no longer with us, and uncovering the truth about his past has become imperative. His complex history, and multiple families, each kept in the dark about the others, are unsettling and dangerous. Everyone, I mean, both Alistair and others, has directed me to you for insight. I implore you, Henry— there's much at stake for Shiloh and myself. Your name keeps cropping up, and I assume you hold information that's helpful to us."

"What do you mean by everyone?" He queried with a raised eyebrow.

I took a deep breath and closed my eyes, praying for strength. The man before me was like a stranger. I can't believe we came from the same womb. We're so different. But I need to be wise now and careful if I want to know more about Ashley's family. And I haven't even mentioned the *Sons of Nephilim.* This wasn't about me anymore. If everything Florence said was true, I needed Henry more than he needed me. I don't even think he does. Mum always said the truth never hurts. So I told him everything.

I stared at him and then lowered my eyes, cutting a picture of distress and pity and praying that would touch a nerve in him. When I met his gaze again, I saw his tight jaw had relaxed, and his eyes had softened. I may have got through to him, but I wasn't so sure.

I paused, watching his reaction, but there was nothing. He had a guarded expression but was listening to my story. So I continued in the same subdued voice.

"I have contacted two of his former wives, and they were cooperative. I still have two more women to call. But during my investigation, Florence said you might know important information about Ashley, and as I said earlier, Alistair also said the same thing. So, I am begging you, Henry, my life, and Shiloh's are in danger if I don't sort this out. And so, your question about everyone is this: Your name keeps coming up, and I want you to help me, please." I was spent and couldn't add anything to it anymore. The ball was now in Henry's court.

A heavy sigh escaped Henry's lips, and I sensed his internal struggle.

Finally, he said, "I can share what little I know about his lineage," he conceded. "Ashley was born in Durban, South Africa. I did some research before you two got involved. I even tracked down his birth mother, Dikelede, who holds a rather unfavourable opinion of him—she referred to him as a cursed child."

My heart sank slightly; I had hoped for more substantial insights. "Is that all?" I asked, a tinge of disappointment in my voice.

Henry hesitated, then spoke again. "There was always something strange about Ashley," he said. "When I returned to see Dikelede, I found an old woman in the family home who said Ashley's birth mother died in a house fire in Nyanga, Zimbabwe. I suspected foul play and contacted the authorities, but nothing came of it. They weren't very helpful. So it was either Dikelede didn't want to see me again or was truly dead. Before I left the old woman, she gave me a note."

Intrigued, I leaned forward. "What did the note say?"

Henry's eyes looked tired as if recounting these memories weighed heavily on him. He spoke slowly, "The note said, *'The child you're searching for is not of this world. He's a trinity of darkness. A demon in three.'* I thought it was nonsense and pursued every lead I could, but the trail went cold. There was no concrete evidence of Ashley's father, just speculation about a Danish immigrant. It was as if his origin was a mystery."

I stared at Henry, struggling to process what he told me, feeling confused and in disbelief. "A trinity of darkness?" I repeated incredulously.

"That's what the note said," Henry confirmed. "I can't explain it, but there was always something off about Ashley, like he didn't belong here, like he wasn't entirely human. It's a feeling I had. My time in South Africa only deepened that suspicion."

While Henry was talking, the puzzle pieces in my mind started to rearrange themselves. Ashley's unknown past, his preference for multiple families, and the narrative of the "trinity of darkness" all fit together. A veil was lifted in my mind, revealing a truth that defies logic and reason. The *Sons of Nephilim, a name that remains unspoken but ominous, held the potential to reveal even more sinister truths.* My journey to find answers had just begun, and the path ahead was uncertain. Impulsively, I shared with Henry everything Florence had said, except for the part about the

Sons of Nephilim. As I did, his grey eyes darkened, and his face turned pale, as if he had seen a ghost.

"So," I added, my voice tinged with urgency, "Ashley was a triplet, and that cryptic mention of a 'demon in three' or a 'trinity of darkness' is unsettling. What are your thoughts on this?"

I observed Henry's trembling right hand and resisted the urge to offer comfort. He was a private man, and I respected that. I wasn't sure if he had a partner or girlfriend; he kept those aspects of his life guarded. He was notoriously cagey about things like that and had always been.

"I'm not certain what to make of it yet," he replied as he settled back into his seat, and we resumed our conversation. I noticed the shift in him. Henry seemed more engaged, showing genuine interest in the details about Shiloh. We discussed for hours, making progress. But I was still hesitant to ask him about the *Sons of Nephilim*. Although it was on my mind, the timing wasn't right. I found it remarkable that Henry opened up to me with a sincerity I hadn't witnessed in years. The chasm that had divided us was slowly closing, and a glimmer of hope began its slow ascent in my heart. Perhaps, just perhaps, this could mark the beginning of healing and reconciliation.

I noticed Henry's sharp reaction to the revelation about Ashley being a triplet. It seemed to catch him off-guard, and I couldn't help but wonder why. At one point, he stood up, pacing the room with his hands clasped behind his back, a furrow forming on his brow. It was a strange sight, reminiscent of my father's mannerisms. I resisted the impulse to mention it, knowing Henry hated being compared to him.

A humming sound emanated from the adjacent doorway, followed by the jarring ring of my phone. Lola's name flashed on the screen, and I glanced at my wristwatch: 9:47 PM. London was six hours ahead of Huntsville, and I wondered at the unexpected call, my heart racing with concern. Shiloh should be home with Lola by now. The call was my cue to return to the hotel, which I relayed to Henry, who was watching me.

Answering the call, Lola's voice quivered with urgency. Her words shocked me – my house was engulfed in flames, firefighters were battling the inferno, and a neighbour had alerted her. The weight of her words took a moment to register fully.

My hands trembled, mirroring the chaos that had entered our lives. "How's Shiloh?" I whispered, the fear of my son threatening to overwhelm me.

"He's safe," Lola assured me, her voice audible but shaky. "But the FBI is here, Christine. I'm outside the house. There are news crews, too. They've found... human remains. You need to come back!"

The trembling shifted from my hands to my entire body. "I'm on my way," I responded, my voice filled with anxiety.

The humming sound persisted, and Henry moved closer to me. Too close. He looked worried.

"Who was that?" he asked, his expression taking on a peculiar quality that I couldn't quite place. Anxiety clawed at me, but I knew that panicking wouldn't help.

"It was Lola," I responded, feeling Henry take the phone from my quivering grasp.

The humming grew louder and three men entered the room, all dressed in black overalls with obscured faces. My gaze locked onto Henry, imploring an explanation.

Henry's attitude seemed troubled, even fearful, as he addressed the men in a rapid stream of Ge-ez and Aramaic. I recognised the language because Mum had taken me to Ethiopia three times. Their obedient nods in response only deepened my sense of bewilderment. Then he ushered me out of the room, guiding me down a lengthy corridor and a flight of stairs. I strained to process the situation, grappling with a sense of foreboding. *My house is on fire with human remains? How can that even be possible? There was no one in the house, and it was empty!* I thought in despair as we ascended the stairs. My attention turned to the walls adorned with peculiar pictures of ancient-looking, bearded men, some of whom bore a striking resemblance to monks. One image even seemed to morph into Shiloh's face, and I screamed, surprising Henry and me. He reacted swiftly, clasping his hand over my mouth, and his other hand urged me up the stairs. We reached a landing, and he kicked open a door, guiding me toward a room.

The room's stark decor further disoriented me. It was a melding of eras, a fusion of ancient and modern, akin to stepping into a time warp. The walls were padded and soundproof, lined with shelves laden with scrolls and worn manuscripts. Movement caught my eye, and I saw a thin, stooped figure with a shock of white hair and glasses perched on his narrow nose. Dressed in the same drab attire as the men downstairs, this man exuded an aura of profound age and wisdom.

The man's cold stare passed over me, and he moved on, disappearing into the recesses of the bookshelves. I refocused on Henry, attempting to maintain an appearance of calm. "May I have my phone back? I need to be with my son. My house is on fire, and they found human remains. The FBI would be interested in speaking to me. I have to be on a flight back home tomorrow. I need answers, Henry."

He let out a heavy sigh, his grey eyes gleaming, and then he dropped a bombshell. "I'm afraid I cannot let you go, Christine. Don't worry about Shiloh. My men are on their way to him. He's safe."

"Your men?" I groaned, the situation veering out of my control. "Could you at least tell me what's going on?"

In response, Henry gestured for me to follow him, and we entered another room, where a hive of activity unfolded before us. Many people stood before screens, engrossed in their tasks. The scene felt straight out of a thriller. And there, on the screen, was Shiloh.

My heart constricted as I watched my son on display, standing outside our burning home, his distress palpable. Lola clutched his hand, attempting to provide solace.

A surge of panic coursed through me, and I turned to Henry, searching for answers. His face bore a strange expression, and I hissed through gritted teeth, "What have you done? How do you have access to this?" And reality dawned on me. Henry has been monitoring my son using a camera drone, or how else could he have been able to capture a live event in my house, far away in Huntsville? And why?

He said nothing, his focus locked onto the screen, until a black van hurtled into view, its door swinging open. A hooded figure darted out and snatched Shiloh, swift as lightning. In an instant, my son was bundled into the vehicle, and it sped away, Lola futilely chasing after it. A flurry of activities followed as the FBI in front of my house also jumped into their cars in hot pursuit of the van, and the room erupted with jubilation and cheers, resembling a control centre during a high-stakes operation. The men slapped each other on the back, and the women hugged. It was similar to a NASA control room.

Dizziness threatened to overwhelm me, and I swayed on my feet. Henry finally noticed my distress, his grip steadying me as he addressed his team. "Well done, everyone. A successful operation."

They exchanged smiles while Henry guided me back to the quieter chamber, what I now referred to as the "Stone Age" room. In the corner, I sank into a leather chair, my energy depleted. My stomach protested loudly, and hunger pangs churned in my insides. Shiloh was now with 'Henry's henchmen'. There was nothing I could do, at least for now. I had to play along. My brother had organised the unthinkable, snatching my son and holding me captive.

Henry's voice cut through the chaos of my thoughts, drawing my attention back to him. "I'm impressed, Christine," he said, his tone measured. "You've evolved from the privileged individual I once knew to a mother fiercely protecting her child." He paused, looking for a response I could not offer. His words continued, each one like a slow-burning revelation. "I promise to reveal the truth you seek. But first, you need to eat. My housekeeper has prepared a late dinner for us."

What a day this has been. My senses were overwhelmed by the dramatic turn of events, the uncertainty surrounding Shiloh, and the surreal surroundings. My stomach grumbled audibly, a reminder of my own needs. A petite woman wheeled in a trolley laden with steaming plates, and although I was hungry, the sight of food soured in my stomach. The genuine desire to be reunited with Shiloh and Lola eclipsed any physical needs. Why would I want to eat without speaking to my son and best friend?

Henry noted my hesitation. "You need food for the challenges ahead."

A surge of frustration bubbled within me. "What challenges? Where is my son? You can't just kidnap a child in broad daylight and not expect any consequences!"

My voice grew louder, my concern pushing aside any restraint I might have held. The memory of Shiloh's anguished cries stayed with me. Lola's repeated warnings had been ignored. In hindsight, perhaps I should have heeded them and stopped my relentless pursuit of information about Ashley after meeting Jane. But I kept unearthing secrets, exhuming ghosts of immense proportions. What was going to happen next?

"I didn't kidnap him. After all, he's my nephew!" Henry insisted, visibly frustrated and defensive. "My actions were driven by a desire to protect both of you. The danger in Huntsville, over returning home—it's all too real."

His words hung in the air, and for a moment, we allowed the comfort of silence. I had nothing to say about Henry's outburst but needed explanations. The only certainty was that I had to persevere. Shiloh's well-being hung in the balance. As if he read my mind, Henry relented, his expression softening.

"Listen, I'll tell you everything you need to know, but first, you must eat," he proposed, a gesture loaded with a hint of care. "And I'll return your phone as well."

I nodded in reluctant agreement, and the housekeeper, an inconspicuous presence until now, approached with a plate. Surprisingly, the food was tasty, and I ate quickly, washing it down with water. Henry, on the other hand, took his time eating. I sat patiently, my foot tapping an erratic rhythm on the floor. Once he had finished, the housekeeper quietly wheeled the food trolley out, leaving us alone.

"Tell me, Henry, are you part of the *Sons of Nephilim*?" I blurted out, asking what had plagued my mind since Florence told me about the group. The strange men downstairs and everything about Henry reeked of a cult.

In response, Henry abruptly rose from his seat, and his face registered different emotions—sadness, frustration, and resignation all woven together.

"Who told about the Nephilim? I thought you'd want to know when you'll see Shiloh." He asked, and I noticed his long eyelids, an extraordinary thing for a man to have such delicate eyelashes.

"He's safe, isn't he?" I countered back. "You just told me my son was safe with strangers I've never met, under the instructions of a brother I haven't seen for almost a decade! How stupid am I?"

Henry's eyes met mine, and his expression conflicted with the same emotions he struggled with earlier. I didn't know what to expect, so I waited.

"Let me start the story from the beginning," he said with a hint of sadness in his voice. "I suspected Dad was murdered and Mum had an extraordinary heritage." His words were a deliberate pace that echoed the gravity of his revelations as he stared at me, and his lips quivered. "I was once well-established within the *Sons of Nephilim*, and they're a very dangerous organisation with archaic beliefs, but I severed ties with them, forging a new path. This will be a long night, Christine.

"Dad's murder? He died of a brain aneurysm, didn't he? You once belonged to that secret organisation?" I asked the barrage of questions with a sudden intake of breath.

Henry shook his head slowly and sat beside me, holding my hands, and his expression was grave.

PART SEVEN

THE GATEKEEPERS

Henry fulfilled his promise by returning my phone. While I dialled Lola's number, he fixed his gaze on me as I answered, her voice a chaotic blend of hysteria, obscenities, and tears. She shared her doubts, surprised by my apparent calmness concerning Shiloh's disappearance. Lola insisted I return home and demanded that I board a plane at once. But Henry had cautioned me not to reveal any information about Shiloh and reminded me that the FBI was involved. So, I said nothing to Lola but promised to return home soon.

It was a difficult call.

I found it tough talking to Lola. I had to make up a story, something I hadn't done since fifth grade. I told her I couldn't change my flight, but she didn't quite believe me. I had to go along with what Henry had advised, even though I still doubted him. Henry also said he would help me find a lawyer if the FBI started asking questions. I was curious about the human remains, but Lola told me I had to be patient and wait for answers. After we finished talking, I tried calling Jane multiple times, but she didn't answer. I made a mental note to try again tomorrow.

I felt stifled, grappling with the oppressive atmosphere of the room; an unexpected surge of claustrophobia took hold, the walls seeming to constrict around me. Henry's presence made things more complicated and made me doubt his intentions. I told him I needed to get some air. He nodded, stood up, and we left the room. Henry led the way down the stairs through his kitchen and the garden. It was now past midnight, and the moon was out. It was chilly, but the fresh air was a welcome relief.

The garden was lovely and big, with smooth paths and trees casting cool shadows. There were chairs where you could sit and relax. But when I looked around, I saw two guards standing near the trees. They had guns, and I realised things might be more serious than I had thought. The peaceful garden now seemed dangerous, and I understood the gravity of my situation.

"Don't worry about the guards," Henry said gently. "I was attacked last month by the SON."

"Sons of Nephilim?" I asked.

He confirmed my suspicion by nodding, gesturing for me to sit among the garden chairs.

"What happened?" I asked with concern, still on my feet.

"It's a story for another time. After the attack, I got a permit to carry firearms and hired these ex-military guys," he replied, motioning towards the two men.

Though brief, the explanation sufficed. Henry noticed a shiver coursing through me, prompting him to direct one of the men to fetch blankets. The man came back and handed over a thick blanket. Draped in their comforting warmth, I settled into a seat, Henry mirroring me from across. The moonlight was agreeable to his form, and he looked handsome but tired. The contours of laughter etched on his face invited trust, yet caution prevailed until I held Shiloh in my arms.

A curiosity about the men nudged me to stand and approach them, appraising them like artworks in a gallery. The first emanated the air of an ex-marine – a chiselled jaw, resolute eyes, and a sturdy build that invoked a sense of security. He reminded me of what it means to be held in strong arms. The second, lean and taut, bore an aura of latent danger. I wondered about their life history and if they had families, wives, and partners. Speculating about their personal lives felt intrusive, and I swiftly quashed the thought. My focus was simple: Until Shiloh and I were safe, notions of dating held no place in my mind. I went back to my seat.

"So, what do you want to know?" Henry asked gently, trying very hard to make me feel at ease.

"Like you promised, everything. From Dad to the Nephilims. Why and how did you join? The reason you started investigating Ashley. What do you mean by Mum's extraordinary heritage."

Henry took a deep breath and glanced around, perhaps contemplating where to begin his tale. I watched him in anticipation. I will finally get answers to some of the mysteries of my life.

Henry started speaking quietly, and something stirred within me as I listened. This was my brother, and a conviction took root – a certainty that whatever unfolded, he would never inflict harm. Call it intuition, but at that moment, I knew. My brother loved me, and everything he may have done and would do was to protect his family– me and Shiloh. He noticed the transformation on my face and stopped abruptly.

"What is it?" he asked, bewildered.

A smile escaped me as I lunged from my seat, embracing him so tightly that we toppled and landed on the lush grass. Memories surged, recollections of Henry's watchful eye through school, the constant shield around me. My brother's love – an unshakeable truth. With newfound certainty, I pulled him to his feet, his face illuminated by a radiant grin. My brother loved me! And I just knew it: Shiloh would be safe.

Curious about my spontaneity, he asked again, "What was that all about?"

"I love you, Henry, and trust you," I responded, a newfound clarity permeating my words. "Let's just say I've come to my senses."

"Fantastic, Christine! You've just made my life a lot easier," he exclaimed, a broad grin stretching across his face. His eyes rested quickly on the guards, and his enthusiasm dampened for a moment. He seemed to consider returning to the house, but the crispness of the cold air held an irresistible pull, and I had no desire to leave either. My eyes followed his toward the guards, and I could read his thoughts. Except I had a hidden microphone, which I don't, so I'm confident our conversation was shielded from their ears. He understood my wish to linger, and so we stayed.

"As I mentioned earlier," he began softly, his words barely audible above the gentle breeze, "It's best to start from the beginning."

I nodded, encouraging him to proceed with an affirming smile.

"Just before our father's passing, he summoned me to his study. He recounted a biblical story, the tale of Noah and the great flood from Genesis. He also spoke of the Book of Enoch, penned by the patriarch Enoch, the great-grandfather of Noah. Dad shared he had read the entire text and extensively studied it. He told me about the Nephilim, describing them as supernatural and demonic beings. These fallen angels had defied God, engaging in relations with humans and corrupting their DNA. Dad believes the Sons of Nephilim brought about the corruption that made the great flood in Genesis necessary to rid the world of their influence. Dad's theory postulated that these Nephilim were the offspring of fallen angels and humans, giving rise to giants—creatures of evil and terror."

"Forgive my interruption, but are you suggesting that these cultists drew inspiration from a Bible story? My understanding of scripture tells me that these beings were wiped out in the flood," I interjected, my impatience bubbling to the surface. "We're not here for a theological debate. How does any of this relate to present-day Nephilim?"

"If you allow me to finish," he responded firmly, "I'll appreciate it. I want to be completely transparent with you and share everything, but it requires your patience."

I mimicked zipping my lips, committing to listening, and he continued.

"Dad revealed that a close friend and fellow professor had approached him for a secretive meeting. Intrigued, he attended, and that was how he became involved with the Sons of Nephilim. Dad believed that the Nephilim were not destroyed during the flood and that their descendants could pose a potential threat, which led to his involvement with the Sons of Nephilim. The Sons of Nephilim, or SON, traced their origins back to 1500 AD in Germany. They find the children of fallen angels by checking for genetic diseases, DNA abnormalities, mutations, or orphans with unknown parents."

Henry paused, and though I refrained from interrupting verbally, my facial expression likely conveyed my curiosity.

"Questions?" he asked.

"Certainly," I replied, my tone higher before adjusting it. "Your explanation has raised more questions than it's answered. I understand that throughout history—whether during the Inquisition, the Salem Witch Trials, where women accused as witches were burnt at the stake or other instances—societies have been prone to adopting beliefs deemed heretical. People were imprisoned or executed for such beliefs. It's conceivable for societies to fall for ideas or be swayed by notions of fallen angels. However, we're living in the twenty-first century, and I can't grasp how Dad, a Physics Professor no less, could have embraced such a narrative."

Henry sighed, shaking his head before responding.

"What you need to understand is that there are mysteries that exceed our comprehension. Regardless of your beliefs, most governments globally, particularly Western nations, have departments investigating paranormal phenomena—encounters with extra-terrestrials, UFOs, and so on. The Sons of Nephilim boasts a global membership numbering in the millions, backed by substantial financial resources. Evil is a reality, and people's fear of the unknown—the demonic, supernatural and unexplainable—keeps organisations like SON alive. They require a focal point for their ideas, and they all genuinely believe they are safeguarding humanity from divine retribution. It's important to note that the Sons of Nephilim comprise individuals from diverse religious affiliations, so they aren't exclusively a Christian faction."

"But God has already passed judgment on these angels. I've read in the scriptures, Henry, and you should, too. See Jude 6:6, and I quote, *'And the angels who did not keep their positions of authority but abandoned their proper dwelling—these he has kept in darkness, bound with ever-lasting chains for judgment on the great Day.'* So, according to the Bible, God has already dealt with errant angels, and the devil and his demons will eventually face consequences," I pointed out, confident that I had a valid argument.

But Henry's countenance contradicted my confident expression.

"What we are witnessing is not Christianity!" Henry said, his face flushed red. "These individuals thought they were in the midst of a divine war, protecting the essence of humanity. Certain religious groups cause destruction if their holy texts are burned. Remember that poor girl in Nigeria? Have you heard what happened to her?"

I hadn't heard about the story. I don't keep tabs on such events. But I must admit, it was scary to be lynched for mentioning one's faith in this twenty-first century.

"No," I muttered, averting my eyes. Henry seemed agitated and angry for some reason. He continued in the same harsh tone.

"The girl spoke about Christ in a WhatsApp chat with her classmates and faced terrible consequences. A group of religious zealots, in a frenzied state, were offended and ended up hunting her down, filming their gruesome spectacle, and burning her alive. The murderers have not been apprehended and might be protected by a corrupt police force. Violence linked to faith is not a rare occurrence. Christians still face unyielding persecution in Islamic countries, with Nigeria being the epicentre. What's your perspective on this?"

I had no response, but I was following the trail of the discussion. Henry's intent gaze bore into mine until he finally answered his own question.

"It's the fatal consequence of fervent religious convictions. Just as innocent women were burnt and accused of witchcraft, it's the same witch-hunting. An online watchdog group researching this grim state of Christians persecuted worldwide reveals a chilling truth: In Nigeria alone, more Christians die for their beliefs than the entire global count combined. A staggering 14 lives snuffed out daily, on average. Just a glimpse into the horrors wrought by entities like Boko Haram sends shivers down your spine. Consider the history — over six million Jews met their end in the Holocaust. Hitler, that embodiment of evil, singled them out for destruction due to their faith. It's enough to make you believe in demons walking the Earth in human forms. This battle, you see, isn't just about survival. It's about preserving the very essence of our existence. I read the Bible too, Christine, and that was where I found the strength to fight against these organisations who believe they're agents of peace and order."

My heart ached at Henry's words, and I felt his despair. I slowly saw glimpses of his heart and liked what I saw. I had misjudged him for years. Several seconds later, he added. "The Sons of Nephilim believe they're preserving the human race."

"Through murdering innocent people?" I asked with a frown, baffled.

"I'm not the enemy here, Christine!" Henry's voice rose by a decibel. "I am fighting against this dangerous ideology. Karl Salzburg, the Monk who started the order in 15th-century Germany, was dogged in his conviction. Some members of SON even claimed that Karl was himself a fallen angel discovered in a field by a wealthy merchant and his wife in 1479 in Eisleben. When they found him, he was rumoured to be aged ten, and his presence was concealed. He was home-schooled by his adoptive parents, who were devout Christians, and when Karl was twenty, he chose the path of a monk. Some accounts say he had a revelation about his true identity and sought a way to reconcile with God. Hence, his mission became the extermination of every remnant of fallen angels and their descendants. It was alleged that Karl believed fallen angels were anomalies that must be pursued and eliminated to prevent further contamination of humanity. There were even dissenters among the Nephilim, members who rebelled against their ideology. In the present day, the organisation uses DNA analysis, claiming that descendants of fallen angels tend to be tall and bear a specific defective gene found in most cancer cells—the mutant p53 gene. This genetic composition is almost universally present in suspected descendants of fallen angels."

"What is the mutant p53 gene? I'm not familiar with it," I said, realising I was entering the unfamiliar scientific territory.

Henry took a deep breath and smiled, but it didn't reach his eyes.

"Mutant p53 is a modified gene that prevents cancer development. However, in many cancer cases, this p53 gene has mutations that mess up its ability to function properly. These mutations often happen in a specific part of the gene, causing problems in how it folds and attaches to DNA. Because of these changes, mutant p53 can't do its job of controlling genes that stop cancer growth. Instead, it ends up being produced in large amounts within tumours. Researchers think fixing or reactivating this mutated p53 could help trigger natural cell death in cancer cells, effectively eliminating them. Interestingly, in suspected descendants of fallen angels, mutant P53 replicates rapidly without causing cancer, which was strange. It's a dual-edged sword, but the descendants of fallen angels exhibit a distinct pattern: they're never sick or harmed by the proliferation of mutant p53. Scientists in the SON are grappling with the reasons for this abnormal DNA due to genetic mutations in the progeny of fallen angels. Mutations in the p53 gene are associated with a higher risk of developing certain types of cancer, even though the gene can also prevent cancer. Another puzzling is that suspected descendants of these fallen angels have good health despite p53, and descendants of these fallen angels possess robust health despite chronic anaemia. However, not all individuals bear these p53 gene mutations. To reiterate," Henry's intense gaze held mine, "mutant p53 is more commonly found in cancer cells themselves rather than in the normal cells of a healthy individual."

"So, some people can have abnormal DNA because of genetic mutations or variations," I said, piecing together the complex information Ashley told me.

"Yes," he agreed with a glint of satisfaction in his eyes. "Genetic mutations are changes that occur in the sequence of DNA, which can lead to alterations in how genes function. These mutations can be inherited from parents or acquired during a person's lifetime due to environmental factors or errors during DNA replication. And as far as the Nephilim were concerned, fallen angels altered the DNA of humanity when they mated with women. These genetic mysteries trouble the Sons of Nephilims, and they're determined to rectify those anomalies ruthlessly."

I sighed. Everything seemed so complex. The concept of the mutant p53 gene seemed far more intricate than anything I had encountered before. Given my lack of expertise in science and genetics, it was beyond my grasp. I limited my talents to managing finances, not deciphering intricate scientific mysteries. I found myself without a response as the reality of his words resonated—an innate fear of the unexplained was a fundamental aspect of human nature.

Then, a thought struck me.

"One question," I said, and Henry raised his eyebrows, attentive.

"Why did the organisation name itself after the very beings they want to eradicate?"

"Good question," Henry's smile reached his eyes this time. "One member reported that Karl Salzburg had written in his journal that he chose the name deliberately to remind the members of their mission and the nature of their adversaries—the Sons of Nephilim, the descendants of fallen angels."

"Even though Karl himself supposedly belonged to that very heritage?" I asked, my brow furrowing.

"Yes," Henry confirmed.

"Perhaps we should return indoors," he suggested, glancing at the guards. Without objection, I stood, silently agreeing. We left the garden and re-entered the room we had temporarily left. Henry asked if I wanted to rest for the night and continue our conversation in the morning, but I declined. The house was now quiet, devoid of the previous activity. Presumably, the individuals from his 'command room' had gone to their quarters and respective homes.

Henry sat behind an imposing oak table, and he invited me to join him. I refused, instead choosing the leather chair where we had shared lunch earlier. I stifled a yawn. Fatigue was undeniable, but my desire for closure regarding this hidden fragment of our family history, brought to light by Ashley's death, was paramount.

Ashley.

For the first time in two months, thoughts of him didn't dominate my mind. Another topic had taken precedence— family.

Clearing my throat, I signalled my readiness for Henry to continue his narrative, and he complied. His grey eyes were like limpid pools, hinting at secrets ready to be laid bare. The surge of affection in the garden seemed to have forged a newfound understanding between us. I meant it— I loved my brother. A decade of bitterness dissolved in the face of the revelations he was about to expose.

I absorbed Henry's words as he peeled back the layers of our family's hidden history.

"Dad's involvement with the SON continued without our mother's knowledge, and he invited me to their meetings. I accepted, and this continued for a year. This clandestine meeting was exhilarating at first. I encountered a plethora of intriguing individuals. However, things slowly went downhill when I started researching and realised the scale of atrocities perpetuated by the organisation: abductions of families, arson, murders, kidnappings and even manipulation of governments worldwide. The most chilling realisation was that former presidents, senators, and influential politicians were among the members. Virtually every tier of government had at least one or two representatives. And then came the chilling truth—Dad ascended to the 'Inner Sanctum,' the highest honour conferred upon a member. However, an exhaustive DNA analysis of inducted members and their families was mandated. Guessed what happened."

I kept quiet because Henry knew my disdain for guessing games. He exhaled, his expression laden with regret. "I apologise," he murmured, his eyes locked into mine. "I remember your strong loathing of guessing games."

"I'm glad you remembered,' I replied, eager for him to continue.

The tension in the room swelled as Henry's next words sliced through the heavy atmosphere. "Dad had no choice but to tell Mum, and that was when all hell broke loose," he admitted with a weary sigh. The gravity of his revelation pressed against me like a weight, and I braced myself for the storm that was about to be unleashed.

"She insisted our father sever ties with the SON, but he refused. Instead, he seized a lock of our hair and submitted it for analysis. The results that returned were nothing short of explosive. Mum's genetic makeup bore the mark of the mutant p53. A revelation that sent tremors through me when I heard. My mind reeled at the implications. Also, a deep dive into her medical history exposed an unnerving absurdity—a chronically low blood count that should have heralded countless illnesses, but Mum was rarely sick. She remained untouched by ill health. The results formed an unsettling picture, one that defied all rational explanations. The revelation bore the weight of a curse, painting us as the descendants of beings beyond human reckoning. Our very existence had been thrust into the throes of uncertainty, our lives compromised by forces we couldn't comprehend."

My eyes widened in shock, my mouth agape. Mum was of German and Ethiopian descent, and if she was linked to fallen angels, it implied that Henry and I were susceptible targets for this ruthless organisation. I closed my eyes briefly, overwhelmed by the gravity of the narrative. Henry perceived my reaction, but he continued nonetheless, his tone sober.

"The subsequent week, Dad slumped and died during a lecture; I suspected poisoning, but the autopsy attributed it to a brain aneurism."

"The Nephilim were responsible for Dad's death?" I asked, my heart heavy. I stood up, shaking with sorrow and anger. Henry's eyes were red as he struggled to control himself.

He swallowed hard before answering.

"Yes, and years later, probably Mum too, but there was no way I could prove it because the autopsy and hospital we took him to were riddled with members of SON. So you can imagine my fears several years later when you met Ashley, an active case. He was peculiar because no one knew his birth parents, hence the reason I insisted you don't get involved with him." He paused for that to sink in, then added. "Dikelede may not be his birth mother, and her disappearance quelled the possibilities of further investigation"

"You should have convinced me, Henry," I cried, thinking of the pain I must have put him through. Henry stood up and approached me, enfolding me in his arms as I wept. After a while, I pulled away, moving toward the shelves and wiping my tears with the back of my hand. My left hand traced the spines of the ancient manuscripts, the weight of the revelations settling upon me.

"Events spiralled out of control as I investigated Ashley," Henry continued in a broken voice. "I resigned from

Wall Street, establishing a counter organisation, 'The Gate-keepers.' We tracked every ongoing investigation started by the SON, aiming to thwart their efforts. Technically, I remained a member of SON to gain insight into their plans, but they found out and blocked my access to the central database. Consequently, I lost contact with their archives and updates on ongoing cases…"

"That means you're no longer part of the organisation," I interrupted, pushing a hair strand from my face. "Even if you think you were."

"Indeed, though I held onto a façade of membership," Henry admitted.

I sank back into the leather chair, weariness creeping up on me slowly. Across the room, Henry reclaimed his seat behind the imposing oak table, his face dark with emotions.

"Alistair, your family lawyer, was a member of SON," he disclosed.

I involuntarily caught my breath at the revelation, though its implications were not entirely surprising. The puzzle pieces fell into place: Alistair's uncanny ability to manipulate and influence, especially regarding Ashley's numerous relationships. The truth was staggering. It was astonishing I had innocently become trapped in a malicious scheme stage-managed by one of the world's most lethal organisations. My attention had been so singularly fixed on Ashley, my resentment directed solely at Henry, that I had remained oblivious to the sinister undercurrents.

As Henry resumed speaking, his words tumbled in a torrent, as if a dam had broken and the long-guarded secrets came gushing forth.

"I didn't know how the Sons of Nephilim planted Alistair as Ashley's confidant and when he became your family's legal advisor," Henry said. His expression bore the gravity of his disclosures. "Sadie was the daughter of a prominent member of the SON. It was apparent they arranged everything to finish Ashley, and would have succeeded if you hadn't kept on digging for the truth." He stopped speaking to catch his breath.

I watched him, fear welling up inside me, and my mouth went dry. My anxious eyes remained fixed on him as he continued his chilling narrative, and the hairs on my arm stood on end.

"There was a chance that you, Shiloh, and everyone connected to Ashley were all marked for death," Henry said, rubbing his tired face with his right hand.

What Henry had done, and was still doing, required immense courage, and I admired his bravery.

"I planned to keep a careful distance from you to fend off potential attacks," he explained, looking at me. "I led a nomadic life, forming alliances worldwide with individuals whose families had suffered at the hands of the Sons of Nephilim. So you can imagine my shock when you revealed Ashley was a triplet; that opened up new possibilities for even more dangerous assaults."

I was frightened as I considered the far-reaching consequences of this revelation. It suddenly dawned on me that one of Ashley's brothers could very well be Jane's husband and the biological father of her twins. The thought had occurred to me at Florence's house. I was now sure of it. Ashley couldn't possibly be in two places at once, attending the birth of his twin sons while also at the hospital when I gave birth to Shiloh. It defied all logic and reason. I would have the chance to share my discoveries with Jane tomorrow, and I could hardly contain my excitement. The subtle pushes from Florence and Alistair to connect with Henry finally made sense. Alistair's true intentions were darker than I had imagined; he manipulated Shiloh and me, using us as pawns in his dangerous game. The situation had snowballed into an intricate jumble of deceit and intrigue, leaving me grappling to understand everything.

The revelations seemed unending. Our conversation continued into the night, with Henry revealing layers of intrigue that shrouded our family history. I struggled to stay awake as Henry's voice faded into the hazy boundary between sleep and wakefulness as my fatigue overpowered my insatiable curiosity. In the end, I was not conscious of being lifted from the chair, carried, and placed on a soft surface, wrapped by the embrace of sleep.

PART EIGHT

THE BEGINNING OF THE END

I awoke in an unfamiliar, luxurious bed, and panic set in as I screamed. The sound echoed, reverberating in the room, and in the wake of my terror, I heard the rapid approach of footsteps resounding through the silence. The door swung open with force, and Henry, his expression tensed with worry, burst into the room. Memories of the last day began flooding my mind like a torrential downpour. I rubbed my eyes and stifled a yawn, my confusion mingling with the sun's gentle embrace filtering through the large bay window.

Henry's worried eyes met mine as he leaned over me. "Good afternoon, Christine. You truly gave me a scare. Are you alright?"

Embarrassment flushed my cheeks, mortified by my reaction. "I'm sorry," I stammered, feeling the warmth rise in my face. "The last thing I remembered was hearing your voice. Waking up in this bed felt like a leap."

"You were sleeping so peacefully. I didn't want to disturb you," Henry explained, staring at me strangely.

And then, a voice, a familiar and heart-warming sound.

"Mum!" It was my son, Shiloh. He dashed into the room, his energy infectious, as he launched himself onto the bed and into my arms.

"Shiloh! Shiloh, my love!" Tears streamed down my face as we clung to each other.

For precious minutes, we babbled and embraced, overwhelmed by emotions. Eventually, I held him at arm's length, tracing his face and ruffling his hair. It was unbelievable how much he seemed to have grown in the short time I'd been gone.

"Mum, the house burned down!" Shiloh's voice quivered with distress.

"We'll find an even better home," I said, trying to sound casual, masking my emotional attachment to our old house. "Besides," I added thoughtfully, "there were memories I'd rather leave behind in that house."

"But I loved my room and the Spiderman bed." Shiloh lamented.

Henry interjected with a comforting tone, "They craft superior Spiderman beds right here in London, you know." The mention of a new Spiderman bed instantly soothed Shiloh's worries as he embraced me again. Henry shot me a glance, his expression now one of relief, and led Shiloh away from the room.

Outside the room, I heard Henry speaking to his house-keeper. Our future hangs in the balance. I wondered if I'd ever return to Huntsville again; it was now too dangerous.

"I'll be back, mum!" Shiloh said, poking his head back into the room.

"Okay, son," I said with a smile. Watching them go, a sense of gratitude swept over me. Henry had kept my son safe in my absence. Then reality set in as my thoughts turned to Lola. How would I explain Shiloh's unexpected presence in London? The idea of her distress tugged at my heart. I sighed, recognising the complexities of the situation, but will face it one step at a time.

"I'll figure that out when the time comes," I murmured, my thoughts drifting as Henry returned, his expression now grave.

"What's wrong?" My heart quickened its pace, dread creeping in. I must have looked like a mess by now, desperate to return to my hotel, retrieve my belongings, and change into something more comfortable.

"They've identified the remains found in your house," Henry said, he looked miserable and avoided holding eye contact. "It was Jane and her sons."

Stunned silence settled over me, replaced by an over-whelming sorrow. Questions flooded my mind. *Jane and her boys, gone? A sense of guilt and responsibility washed over me like a tide. Why had they been at my house? She knew I was in London. What had led her there?* My hands trembled as I comprehended the gravity of Henry's revelation. Someone had been tracking me, someone who knew intimate details about my life.

Lola? I thought. No. I shook my head vehemently. The thought lingered, but I pushed it aside. Lola was family. She wouldn't betray me. I've known her for 30 years; a life-long friendship couldn't be a facade. But in this uncertain reality, doubt slithered in like a shadow because anything was possible in my upside world.

"Are you sure it was Jane and her boys?" I asked Henry. My voice trembled, and I had problems keeping still.

Henry confirmed this with a solemn nod, settling onto the bed beside me, offering a comforting presence as the truth bore down on me like an avalanche. But the tears refused to fall as I froze in shock. Regret flooded through me and I realised that perhaps digging into Ashley's past had been a grave mistake. Certain secrets were best left buried.

"Someone has been tailing me," I said, stepping away from him, my legs unsteady beneath me. "Someone with complete knowledge about my life. If I hadn't contacted Jane, she'd still be alive."

"We don't know if you hadn't reached out to Jane, she'd still be alive," he said, his eyes sad. Standing up, he walked to the window, his back turned to me, peering down at the street below. When he faced me, I noticed the wrinkles near his eyes. "The Nephilim are merciless, known to shadow families for years before striking. They may have been tailing her for years, and you had the right to know about Ashley, and from our monitored conversations, your quest for the truth was justified."

He turned away from the window. Henry appeared to have aged within twenty-four hours I'd been with him. Deep lines etched on his forehead as he frowned.

His words caught my attention. "You bugged my house!" My anger flared, my sense of violation simmering beneath the surface.

"How else could we have ensured your safety?" Henry's defence was swift, and he moved closer to the door, his stance becoming guarded.

Thoughts of Florence and Angel suddenly rushed in, demanding my attention. I had to warn them. I relayed this to Henry, who told me Florence had already left for Scotland that morning. The realisation dawned upon me—Henry seemed to know everything. Were there any secrets he didn't hold?

"There's something about Lola you need to know," Henry's voice grew softer and his countenance gentler. My heart quickened, sensing a revelation in the air. If Henry confirmed my suspicions, I don't know if my fragile heart could withstand it.

"I want no more secrets between us," he began, his eyes meeting mine with a vulnerability I hadn't seen before. "I've loved Lola since the fifth grade." His confession hit like a bombshell, catching me off guard.

"What?" My exclamation was a mix of disbelief and confusion.

"You and Lola? Does she know?" I asked. My shy brother Henry was in love with my best friend.

"Yes," he replied. "I shared my feelings when she visited London with her husband years ago. It was an unexpected encounter."

"Why are you telling me this?"

"As I promised, no more secrets," Henry replied, unable to maintain eye contact. "We became intimate, and I implored her to keep it from you. Then, three months later, she called to tell me she was pregnant."

My legs wobbled beneath me, and I sank back onto the bed, staring at Henry in disbelief. My best friend Lola and reserved brother Henry—were involved in a clandestine affair. And Lola, she kept this from me? It struck me like a bolt of lightning—Melody, her daughter, could be Henry's. Lola had secrets, too. We always told each other everything, but I was wrong. Too many secrets. Am I the only human without secrets? I wondered. My eagerness to see and confront her grew steadily.

"Oh, my goodness," I murmured, running my hands through my hair. But what would Daniel, Lola's husband, make of this revelation? What if he uncovered the truth?

"Melody, could be your daughter?" I questioned, trying to comprehend the enormity of it all.

Henry nodded, his voice barely above a whisper. "She is. I confirmed it during my last visit to Huntsville. But I'm worried, Christine. If the Nephilims discover the truth, Melody's life could be in danger. That's why I reached out to Lola today."

"You did what?" My astonishment was evident. "You didn't want Lola to know Shiloh was under your care before bringing him to London, but now you've reached out to her?" I shook my head in confusion. "And you came to Huntsville without seeing me or your nephew?"

"Jane's death changed everything," Henry said, his voice heavy with worry. "An FBI contact informed me they were likely killed elsewhere and their bodies dumped in your house. I can't take any chances. I apologise for not visiting you and Shiloh, but it was for the best, ensuring your safety." He rolled up his sleeves to reveal the three-star birthmark on his wrist, mirroring the one on Angel's wrist.

The room felt like it was holding secrets, revelations, and the eerie presence of the Nephilim. I touched my chest, felt the rapid beating of my heart, and anguish filled every fibre of my being. The warmth of the sun turned cold and eerie, mirroring the uncertainty that had taken hold of my life. It was in the moment of Henry's confession that I understood the dangerous, shadowy powers had touched every aspect of my world.

"Ashley and Mum had a strange connection," Henry said with a tremble in his voice and the words came tumbling out without restraint. "The Nephilim were involved somehow, even though I've never bought into the fallen angels' theory. But what if it's true? What if we were under a curse or strange connection?" Henry stared at me. The pain in his eyes was heart-wrenching. I wanted to hug him, but I knew it was better to let him speak from the heart.

"While in Lalibela, Ethiopia, researching our family history," he said and his voice grew faint. I inched towards him and held his hands in a comforting grip. His voice dropped to a murmur. "I met sympathetic monks who shared ancient texts about the Nephilim and fallen angels. I've been studying them, but deciphering the meanings has proven elusive. The accounts are contradictory, each offering different interpretations. The monks told me that Grandad appeared in a field one night when he was ten years old. He spoke fluent German and had no memory of how he got to the field. They took him to the German embassy in Addis Ababa, where they confirmed his German roots but did not provide more details. He stayed in Ethiopia, and the priest who discovered Grandad took him home and he lived with the priest's family. Years later, he met Grandma, and they married. Mum was their only child. Those men you saw downstairs yesterday pray at 9 p.m. every night to wade off evil. They're my friends from Ethiopia."

He stopped speaking, his eyes searching for understanding in mine.

"It's alright," I reassured him with a strained smile. "We'll figure this out. You've shown great resilience by protecting Shiloh and me for a decade without arousing our suspicion. I believe in God and evil, even though I'm not on board with the concept of fallen angels interacting with humans. There are mysteries we will never comprehend, as you pointed out yesterday." I stopped to let that sink in.

Henry raised his eyebrows and nodded.

I fixed him with an intent gaze and shrugged. "Perhaps there's an alternate universe out there. Who knows?" I asked with a faint smile. "What matters is the love of family and friends. I saw a documentary where an astronaut discussed the mysteries of our universe. Such as black holes and how their presence still eludes them. We can't *know* everything. And if there was anything I learned from investigating Ashley's history, there are secrets that *will* stay hidden."

"You nailed that speech, little sis," Henry said with a proud smile. "I meant what I said yesterday. You've grown into an incredible woman."

With that, he produced a Ruger semi-automatic pistol from his trouser pocket. "I want you to have this for personal protection. I know Dad got you a gun before he died, but given the threats we face, it's good to have an extra layer of security. I'll take care of getting the necessary permits."

"Thanks," I said with a faint smile. Memories of Jane's death still weighed on me. If I could turn back time, I could have saved her by not contacting her. Then I'll live my simple life and maybe remarry, and Shiloh and I will be safe.

He walked toward the door and turned back. "Lola will be here in the evening with Melody. They're on the flight to London right now."

My hands dropped to my sides.

"What comes next, then?" I asked, astonished. "Lola had a life in Huntsville. Maybe I can uproot and leave behind my past, supported by financial stability. But Lola can't abandon everything and move to the UK. She's still married and has a younger sister who needs her."

Henry walked back and held me by the shoulders; his eyes looked sad, but I also saw determination.

"I've seen countless evil in my forty years, Christine— things you may never understand. I want to tell you everything, but too much information could be detrimental. Lola was an adult and decided to come to the UK based on the information I gave her. I think she also realised that her daughter could be in danger. When she comes, please be kind. She's your best friend, but you've both gone through some traumatic experiences. Processing it all will take time."

"Understood," I agreed. "But for now, I'll head back to my hotel to check out."

"Of course," he said. "You and Shiloh can go together, and security will accompany you. While the Sons of Nephilim might not be a dominant force in the UK, they could strike when least expected."

I sank onto the edge of the bed, the events of the past few days churning around in my mind. The ceaseless influx of information left me drained, a bone-deep weariness settling into my core. Henry had been right all along – an excess of anything, no matter how crucial, could be detrimental. I closed my eyes, attempting to make sense of how quickly my life had changed.

My trip to London was a simple, fact-finding mission. I expected it to last a week. Within that short period, my world as I knew it had shattered. Jane and her sons were murdered. I shuddered at the pain they went through and the floodgates opened, my tears fell in torrents.

I wept for those innocent boys. Their dreams are cut short. My chest heaving with pain, my eyes shut as I went through the shock of their loss. My body shook as pain racked through every fibre of my being. The tears fell as memories of Jane's beautiful face assailed my mind. I wept for her broken dreams, never to be realised. After ten minutes of violent weeping, I flopped back on the bed, exhausted. My mind went back to Henry and Lola.

My brother's relationship with my best friend was an unpredictable rollercoaster. Her daughter, Melody, was now part of our unconventional family dynamic. My palms were wet and clammy with fear. My body was hot and I started sweating at the problems we faced. Where do we start again? I knew Henry had plans, but I hated being kept in the dark. My mother and Ashley shared a weird heritage. My brother had taken on the role of a "Gatekeeper" and made it his mission to protect innocent people from a false prophecy that lacked divine endorsement.

Because of the chaos, I found myself without a home. Forced to live on the run while eluding the relentless pursuit of this faceless cult. My exhaustion was profound, and I yearned for a glimpse of normalcy, a relief from the difficult incidents that now defined my existence. In my weariness, a spark of anticipation ignited within me – the prospect of reuniting with Lola. Perhaps together, we could chart a course for the next chapter of our lives.

In the mayhem, a semblance of relief managed to penetrate the storm clouds that loomed over me. Lola's loyalty to me had not wavered. This simple fact provided comfort in a world where trust was increasingly rare. She had not betrayed me, and for that, I was grateful.

Leaving the confines of the room behind, I went downstairs. I entered the lower floor and noticed Shiloh following his uncle everywhere with an exuberant enthusiasm that only a young child could muster, tailing Henry's every step. I had a quick lunch, left the house, and went to the hotel.

The journey itself was uneventful, a mundane sequence of events. I was alert, my eyes darting towards the rearview mirror of the Audi Q7, a cautious attempt to detect any signs of a pursuing vehicle. I was relieved when we returned to the safety of Henry's residence.

Stepping inside the house, a scene unfolded that disturbed me. We saw many people downstairs, an unexpected congregation that put Shiloh and me on the defensive. Sensing the need for a retreat, we sought refuge in the library, where we stumbled upon Henry. An array of documents spread before him. Our entrance brought a shift in the atmosphere. His face lit up when he saw us.

"It's a full house downstairs," I said with an uneasy smile, understanding Henry's lifestyle and thankful for his dedication. He was committed to saving innocent people from the clutches of the SON. Without his timely intervention, Shiloh and I could be dead.

"Yeah, sorry, I should have warned you," he drawled with a wide grin. "This place is like an embassy for people like us."

"Thanks for all you do," I said, my eyes moist.

"It's alright, anything for my little sis and favourite nephew," he replied affectionately.

"Oh, Mum," Shiloh turned to me, his eyes bright. His time in London seemed to invigorate him. "Thanks for sending Eric and James to fetch me from the house. I thought I was being kidnapped," he added, his youthful wit present. Thankfully, my brain connected, and I managed a smile, glancing at Henry for support.

"Yes, your mum wanted you out of there. She's quite the superhero," Henry chimed in, laughter punctuating his words.

"May I explore your house?" Shiloh asked, smiling, his face brimming with curiosity. He looked so happy, and I prayed everything would work out as I searched for a new place to live in the UK. Henry's residence was a six-bedroom detached house brimming with people. It's not for an average, boisterous child like Shiloh, but he appeared to thrive in the activities and interactions. He was talking to everyone, laughing and asking questions. How could someone in their right senses want to harm such a harmless child?

The sound started as a murmur and gradually got louder. Henry's eyes widened at a brief admission of fear before determination set in. Gunshots erupted, their thunderous echoes reverberating throughout the house.

We're under attack.

Henry pulled me and Shiloh close, and then he deftly pressed a concealed button behind the bookshelf. A door opened, revealing a passage, and he guided us inside.

"Go down the stairs and into the room by your right. Please, don't make any sound. I'll come to you. Regardless of what happens, don't come out," Henry instructed, a dark gleam in his eyes.

Shiloh, surprisingly composed, tightened his grip on my hand.

"Stay safe, Henry!" I whispered, my voice trembling with fear. He pressed a finger to his lips, blowing us a fleeting kiss.

We followed Henry's directions, the sound of running footsteps echoing from above. This was our reality now— a life perpetually under siege. Henry closed the door, and we went down the stairs. It was like an underground bunker. We walked briskly and saw the room. It was small and bare. Entering, we bolted the door but still heard running steps above us.

Shiloh clung to me, and I held him tightly. The silence was suffocating, the tension very real. He will be ten years old soon, and I can't hide the truth from him any longer.

"Hey, son," I said calmly, "I'll always be here for you."
 Silence.

"I *know*, Mum," he said, at last, holding me tighter. "I wished there was something I could do to protect you and Uncle Henry."

"We do the protecting, Shiloh, not you," I whispered, my heart aching for my young son, who was forced to confront such dangers. "Although we can't always prevent bad people from trying to hurt us, be rest assured, they won't succeed."

"I know, mum, I know." He agreed, and there was silence again.

Half an hour later, I made a life-changing decision. Softly, I murmured his name, "Shiloh," my voice full of emotion and sorrow. There was a fleeting pause, and he responded with a fragility that seemed at odds with his young age. "Yes, Mum?"

"I need you to listen carefully," I said in a thin, nervous voice, my eyes locking onto his, ensuring an unbreakable connection.

His earnest nod was accompanied by eyes brimming with unshed tears.

"Promise me, darling, that you won't open this door for anyone except me and Uncle Henry," I pleaded, staring at him. "It's important, Shiloh."

"Yes, Mum," he said in a stronger voice. "I promise."

I gave him a quick kiss as the earsplitting echoes of gunfire pierced the air once again, a stark reminder of the danger upstairs, and my brother was fighting, alone, with men who would die for him.

I needed to be there.

As the battle raged on, fear and willpower churned within me. The situation was fraught with uncertainty, but I steeled myself for the challenges that lay ahead.

I left the safety of the room, returning to the fray, my steps heavy with the reality of what could happen if I did nothing. The thought of leaving Shiloh alone gnawed at me, but I would not forgive myself if anything happened to

Henry. After years of missed opportunities, I had to fight for him the same way Henry protected me and Shiloh.

I knew Henry was skilled in combat, unlike me, though I, too, had honed my marksmanship skills when I attended shooting ranges with Dad.

I gritted my teeth and prepared mentally, blood pumping through my veins in intensity. Each gunshot marked the rhythm of my heartbeat, and I evaded imaginary, flying bullets by stooping low. I climbed the stairs and reached the landing, pushing the door open and was met with a barrage of bullets. I ducked, finding refuge beneath Henry's massive oak table. From this vantage point, I spotted two attackers charging into the library. My aim was accurate as I targeted their legs. Shots from the Kruger semi-automatic pistol Henry gave me earlier finding their mark. They crumpled to the ground with a thud, their agonised cries filling the air. Emerging from my cover, I silenced them with point-blank shots, releasing my pent-up frustration and anger.

In those moments, I had taken two lives to save mine.

Gathering their weapons, my hands trembling with adrenaline, I prepared to leave the library. However, my attention was drawn to a figure whose leg protruded from a fallen bookshelf. Gritting my teeth, torn between duty and compassion, I went back and knelt beside the wounded man. It was the same old man I saw in the library yesterday. I lay down the attacker's weapons and cradled his head, assessing the severity of his injuries. Blood seeped from wounds on his neck and chest, his chances of survival uncertain. His eyes met mine, an intense connection that seemed to pierce my soul. I attempted to move him, but his pained grunts prevented me, so I shifted him gently out of sight, shielding him from prying eyes.

He mouthed, 'Thank you,' before his eyes fluttered shut. His breath ceased, and his chest stilled. Anguish swelled within me as an unnecessary death weighed heavily on my conscience.

I retrieved the weapons and moved stealthily towards Henry's last position. In the chaos of gunshots and Henry's commanding shouts, my focus was singular—I had to reach him. Following his voice, I located him, pinned down under a barrage of fire. Our eyes locked, and his plea to stay back resounded.

"Get back. I told you to stay away!"

"I won't," I retorted defiantly, a sense of duty and love propelling me. "Who's going to stop me?"

With my back pressed against the wall, I caught sight of movement from the corner of my eye. An assailant had out-flanked us. Instinct guided my aim, using the enemy's CVA.300 Cascade rifle, shots ringing out in rapid succession. The assailant faltered, dropping his weapon to the ground, his demise a testament to my unerring accuracy.

But our triumph was fleeting as the room erupted in renewed gunfire. Our adversaries were relentless. In our exchanged glances, Henry and I shared an unspoken pact to stand firm. Though outnumbered and outgunned, we refused to yield. The hallway had transformed into a battleground, my resolve to reach Henry unyielding.

A barrage of bullets tore into the wall beside me, the sound of splintering wood a stark reminder of my precarious situation. Moments later, a rapid volley of shots echoed above, mingling with shouts and chaos. Henry signalled toward the library, a silent command to retreat to the underground bunker. I complied swiftly, renewed hope surging within me. The tide had shifted.

I raced back to the library, grabbing the documents Henry had been poring over, conscious of their vital importance. Rushing to the hidden door, I glanced around, ensuring my brother's safety. With the door sealed, I descended the stairs to the refuge below.

My fists hammered against the door.

"Shiloh, open up. It's Mum."

The door swung open, revealing a young man marked by the weight of violence witnessed too soon. I dropped the documents and enveloped him in a hug.

"I promised I'd return," I reassured him, a smile tugging at my lips as I ruffled his hair.

"I knew you would," he replied, his eyes seeking confirmation. "How's Uncle Henry? Is he alright?"

"He's alright," I replied, a mixture of affection and resilience in my tone, picking the documents with my right hand, my left on Shiloh's shoulders. "He might not show it, but I lent him a hand. He'll be back soon."

We waited. Minutes were like hours, and the ordeal left us exhausted. We must have dozed off as a loud knocking on the door jolted me awake. Shiloh and I got to our feet, and I pressed my hand against the gun hidden in my back pocket. The voice outside identified itself as Lola's, but I hesitated. Henry had warned us not to open the door for anyone but him.

"Where's Henry?" I asked cautiously. There was no answer.

"Is that you, Henry?" I asked, louder this time.

"No, it's me, Christine. Lola!" Her voice was shaky.

Shiloh and I exchanged glances, Henry's warning echoing in my mind. Open the door solely for him, it emphasised. Even Lola, my dearest friend, was subject to that condition.

"Where's Henry?" I asked firmly.

"I'm right behind Lola, Christine. Please, open the door!"

I complied. Lola and Melody entered, followed by Henry. He trailed behind, his condition dire—blood staining his shirt, his hand pressed to his abdomen in a futile effort to staunch the flow. He'd been shot in the stomach. I rushed to his side and grabbed him as he grimaced in pain. Lola's face showed worry and anger.

"You heard my voice, Christine, and you still hesitated?" Her frustration was evident.

I apologised, though my attention remained on Henry. He was in bad shape, and I cursed myself for not opening the door. I wished I'd waited before running back to the library. I wanted to ask what happened but knew there was no time for small talk. His face contorted in pain, his voice scarcely above a whisper. Henry managed a faint smile, his eyes conveying gratitude for my daring move. And at that moment, I knew that our fight against the Sons of Nephilims was far from over. But we were determined to face whatever challenges lay ahead—together.

Weakly, Henry pointed a trembling finger at the back of the room. Lola followed the direction of his finger, saw a button on the wall and pressed it. I gave Shiloh the documents as a door opened, and we rushed to Henry's side; sandwiched between us, we ambled to a Benz jeep parked in what appeared to be a garage. I glanced at Melody briefly, her adorable face wide with fear.

We helped Henry into the back seat, and I sat beside him and Shiloh. Lola jumped in the driver's seat, and Melody sat with her in the front. She horned, opened the garage door remotely through a mobile device in the vehicle, and drove out at high speed, glancing back at Henry. When we were several yards away, Henry pressed a number on the bloodied phone in his hands, and a massive explosion ripped through his house.

I stared at him in shock.

"I'll explain later," he whispered, blood pouring from his mouth.

"Don't talk, Henry," I said softly, my hand resting gently on his arm.

That day marked a turning point—the beginning of the end for the cruel organisation that had sown chaos across millennia, wielding fear as a weapon. Fortunately, Henry survived, though the cost was steep—twenty Gatekeepers perished, including one of his most trusted guards and the old librarian, one of Henry's oldest allies. At least I silenced three of our enemies, I thought with satisfaction, which gave me confidence that I could protect my family from harm. The Sons of Nephilim had tracked Lola and Melody to Henry's residence, raining gunfire upon them. But they underestimated the resolve of the UK to protect its soil. Henry collaborated with MI5 to counter the threat and neutralise the attackers.

Daniel, Lola's husband, was a member of the Nephilim. He had planned harm to Shiloh, coinciding with the same day my house was engulfed in flames. The unfolding events took a significant turn when Henry's call came in. Unknown to Lola, Daniel monitored her conversations by tapping into her phone. As they say, the rest became history. While the SON remains active within the United States, several countries have begun dismantling the organisation, leading to the arrest of its members.

The threat to our lives was still active, but we were safer than before. The trouble was there was always someone left to fight.

PART NINE

A SAFE HAVEN

That cold October in Huntsville, Alabama, changed my life forever. Now it's February, marking five months since. Everything I went through reshaped me. I've become a better woman and a great mother—a fighter. I would save my family with the last drop of my blood. Would I change some experiences? Of course, but my life was now whole and filled with so much happiness.

I stood outside the historic and charming Holy Trinity Church in St Andrews, bathed in the gentle embrace of its timeless beauty. The sky, a vast canvas of cerulean blue, held the sun in its arms, casting a warm and inviting glow upon the scene. I wore a simple, sleeveless blue gown that flowed gracefully, complemented by white heels. My hair cascaded down in intricate tresses, a perfect adornment for the occasion. The atmosphere was one of pure joy, with the whispered blessings of the wind carrying away the lingering shadows of the past.

I looked towards the church courtyard and saw Melody and Shiloh playing hide and seek, their laughter blending with the sound of distant bells. Florence, Angel, and two others walked over with beaming smiles of joy. I rushed to meet them with excitement, and our embrace confirmed the unspoken connection between us. Their presence was a testament to our unity and friendship, a support system that had weathered storms.

We walked into the church and found a seat in a pew near the altar. The ornate interior reflected the importance and solemnity of the moment. The gathering expanded, with attendees dressed in suits and dresses, their dark sunglasses. Most of them were Gatekeepers, Henry's loyal guardians, who stood by him through trials and tribulations. Women I didn't recognise embraced me like an old friend. Henry has saved their lives from the Nephilim, and I was family to them. Every hug and kiss shared was a celebration of life, resilience, and hope for a better tomorrow.

Let me clarify, though, that the day was not about me. I was not the one getting married. Instead, it was Henry, my brother and closest confidant, who had summoned the courage to ask Lola, his beloved, to be his life partner. The long-awaited divorce from her former husband, Daniel, had materialised, clearing the path for this celebration of love.

Ah, Daniel. A wolf in sheep's clothing. He was in the inner circles of the Nephilim, a wicked man who we suspected ordered the killings of Jane and her children. Our intelligence sources among the Gatekeepers had uncovered his sinister motives – marrying Lola to get closer to my parents, a calculated relationship right from the start. I was happy Lola got away from him.

This day, planned over three months, marked the union of two souls as Henry, my brother, and Lola, my best friend, embarked on a journey of matrimony. It was a celebration to remember, a reprieve from the turbulent weeks that had preceded it. Although Henry was hesitant, I had held my ground, convinced that we needed this grand wedding as a moment of respite, a chance to dance, celebrate, and revel in life's beauty.

I left the pew and went outside, and my mind shook off these troubling thoughts, for the day belonged to Henry and Lola. Standing at the church entrance, sunlight streaming through stained glass, I watched Henry arrive, dapper and looking like our father, mischief twinkling in his grey eyes. Our shared glance held a fleeting shadow, a brief reminder of the trials we had endured. Yet, as our hands clasped and his whispered gratitude reached me, the shadows were banished, leaving joy in its wake.

"Thank you." He mouthed the words and entered the church with his best man, a man I'd never seen before, but one of Ashley's contacts in the Netherlands. And then the moment I'd been waiting for arrived.

The ceremony truly began with Lola's arrival in a limousine. She looked exquisite in a cream-coloured wedding gown, an ethereal vision that mirrored the joy in her heart. I went to meet her with a massive smile on my face.

"You look stunning!" I exclaimed, my happiness bubbling over.

Lola was nervous and breathless.

"Do I look alright?" she asked, her voice shaky.

"Of course!" I said with a huge smile. Her eyes were bright with anticipation, I clasped her hands, offering support and reassurance as we walked into the church.

The congregation rose in respect, and the choir's harmonious melodies filled the space, adding a delicate touch to the occasion. I watched in admiration as Lola stood beside Henry, and the service started. Our eyes met briefly, and I was grateful for how far we'd come. Five months ago, I hadn't seen my brother in a decade, and now he was marrying my best friend.

Everyone was filled with joy at the wedding. I took countless photos of Henry's happiness to capture the magic of the day. I wished time could freeze, so this joyous affair could last for a longer time. The festivities ended, as all good things must.

They exchanged vows and went to St Lucia for their honeymoon. They came back and bought a house in St. Andrews. Lola began a PhD in international law while Henry continued expanding the Gatekeepers in Scotland and Europe.

My new home was a charming five-bedroom cottage, nestled in the serene surroundings of LadyBank Hills, a quaint village in the Scottish countryside. The village, embraced by lush foliage and canopy trees, provided a sense of security that echoed the newfound peace of my life. The cottage had a big garden where Shiloh played football after school. He'd adjusted to the local school and made friends. It warmed my heart to see him thriving. I had also rekindled a lost passion: painting. I turned the large shed in my garden into a studio, and it became my sanctuary, spending hours there daily painting. It was a space where I translated my imagination onto the canvas, capturing angels, landscapes, and images of my family. I've created at least ten paintings. Henry had suggested that I ought to consider an exhibition at the prestigious Christie's in New York, but I objected. My art was not for sale. I was painting for myself, not for public scrutiny. I don't want unwarranted attention. People gawking at my creations, critiquing me, and asking silly questions about my inspirations.

I continued researching my family's and Ashley's ancestry online. Two women I met online claimed to know Ashley, but I chose to stop pursuing their stories after Jane's death reminded me to be cautious.

My existence, previously filled with chaos, had transformed into a calm, normal reality. I smile often and have made new friends. After facing hellish trials, Shiloh, Henry, Lola, and Melody are my treasured family and a haven. I felt liberated when I forgave Ashley and my wounds healed, scars fading away. He was a tragic figure, unable to break free from the clutches of his demons, and his life had been marred by circumstances beyond his control.

My life was now filled with peaceful music, composed by the laughter of Shiloh, the warmth of Henry, and the glow of Lola and Melody. I love the rich cultural heritage of Scotland. I love my new country. I chose to stop feeling burdened by Ashley's legacy and instead accepted his imperfections, working towards the redemption he never received.

However, I found it strange that Ashley had only fathered sons and no daughters. There had to be a rationale behind it, but for the time being, I was finished with my investigation. It also felt great to grant him forgiveness. Ashley was just as much a victim as I was — a casualty of life's unpredictability. Sadly, he didn't have a long enough life to correct the errors he had made or to find liberation from his inner struggles.

A newfound presence graced my life: a man named Nathan, the village vicar, and a former soldier. His gentle personality, shaped by his experiences in the battlegrounds of Afghanistan and Iraq, found its way past my defences. Our bond, guarded yet growing, carried traces of hope and companionship. Nathan's spiritual guidance led me to newfound faith, and in the embrace of scripture, I discovered a peace that transcended the turmoil of my past. Embracing the teachings of Jesus Christ, I shed my old identity, reborn with renewed confidence. Talking with Nathan brought healing. I love the slow pace of our relationship. We live one day at a time.

Henry relocated the Gatekeepers' headquarters to St. Andrews and started a local chapter in our village. It was like a charity, and Eric was in charge of it. It was important to be vigilant and protect our peace. The battles of the past were still fresh in our memories. A clear warning of past horrors and the persistent threats that could undermine it was a pointer to be careful.

As the doorbell rang, signalling Shiloh's return from school, my heart leapt with joy. I swung open the door, greeted by his exuberance as he dashed inside, accompanied by his bodyguard, Eric, whom we have woven his presence into our lives, a neighbour with a cover story that shielded the truth. Henry had insisted Eric stay with us. Our neighbours assumed he was family because he lived in the next cottage around the corner with his pit bulls. Eric stayed in the shadows, watching our every move, his presence inconspicuous.

A surprise awaited as Henry and Lola emerged before me, smiles illuminating their faces. Their unannounced visit from St Andrews was a treasured gift, and my heart swelled with contentment. I was happy. If this was not heaven, I don't know what it is.

The afternoon sun streamed through the windows, casting warm hues across the room as the three of us sat down to eat. I decorated the table with an array of dishes: roast potatoes, grilled chicken, and vegetables, and the aroma of the food filled the air. Melody and Shiloh bounded down the stairs and joined us at the table, their faces flushed with excitement.

As we enjoyed the meal, laughter and conversation flowed. We exchanged stories and memories revisited, and the atmosphere was one of genuine joy. It was as if time had stood still, and we were wrapped in the cocoon of friendship and family.

After lunch, we moved to the living room, where the kids played a game while Lola and I found a quiet corner to talk on the sofa. She clasped my hands in hers, and I waited, wondering what she wanted to tell me.

"What's your secret?" I asked, watching Melody and Shiloh as they raced to the garden.

"Henry," we both chorused and burst into laughter. Then a shadow crossed her face.

I questioned her with my eyes, and her hands trailed to her stomach as she held it protectively. I understood her.

"How many months? You guys just got hitched. That was quick!" I touched her cheek. It was warm.

"Eight weeks."

"You've been busy!"

"Oh yeah," she smiled, lowering her eyes as the sun kissed her glowing skin. I love the smooth rays of the evening sun.

Lola looked at me with a frown and said, "I'm nervous about telling Henry."

I placed a reassuring hand on her shoulder. "You know him better than anyone. He loves you, and he's going to be thrilled. Henry's going to be a father again!"

Different emotions played across her face, but a small smile crept onto her lips. "I hope so. It's just that, well, it's a big surprise, and I don't want him to feel overwhelmed. Besides, I still remember the fear in his voice when he called me before we raced out of the house and came to London. He doesn't strike me as a man who wanted a large family." She paused before continuing. "You know, because of the Nephilim."

"It doesn't matter. You're growing love. Two hearts melted into one, and I'm sure Henry will be thrilled. You've both been through so much together," I said, reflecting on their journey. "And you've built a strong foundation. This will only make your bond even stronger. The Nephilim are no longer a threat. Trust me on that."

Lola's eyes sparkled with gratitude. "Thank you for being here for me, for us."

"You are family, Lola," I replied. "You've been there for me, too, and that's what family does."

As the day transitioned into the evening, Henry joined us once again. The room was filled with anticipation and nervousness as Lola looked at him, her eyes filled with love and apprehension. Henry noticed her unease and took her hands in his.

"What's going on?" he asked, his voice gentle with a tinge of worry.

Lola took a deep breath before speaking. "Henry, I have something to tell you."

He squeezed her hands. "You can tell me anything."

After a moment of silence, Lola said with a smile spreading across her face. "I'm pregnant!"

Time stood still for an instant before a look of sheer joy spread across Henry's face. He pulled Lola into a tight embrace, his happiness a sign of relief. I had wondered how Henry would take the news.

"You're serious?" he exclaimed, his voice filled with disbelief and joy.

Lola nodded, tears of relief and happiness pooling in her eyes. "Yes, I am."

Henry kissed her forehead and lips, his happiness radiating throughout the room.

"Lola, you've made me the happiest man in the world."

Laughter and tears mingled as the weight of the revelation lifted, leaving behind a sense of euphoria. The embrace they shared was not physical; it was a celebration of love, trust, and the promise of a new beginning.

As the day drew to a close, we sat together, basking in the warmth of togetherness. The surprise visit brought an unexpected gift that would forever be etched in our hearts—the memory of a day when joy and love converged and heaven felt close.

Henry made his way to the garden where the children were playing. I stole a glance at Lola, contemplating whether it was the right moment to bring up the subject of Daniel. We had avoided discussing it, but my curiosity got the better of me, and I wanted to know Lola's feelings on the matter.

"We've never talked about Daniel," I said, looking at her.

Lola brushed a strand of hair away from her face and met my eyes. "There wasn't much to say," she replied with a shrug. "He wasn't home much, always at the hospital. And I knew you had a lot going on, so I didn't want to add to your problems." She looked down, her voice faltering as emotions seeped through. "The hardest part was realising I was used. Daniel wouldn't have married me if we weren't friends, and that hurt. He wanted to be close to your family through me." Lola closed her eyes, as if remembering, then opened them to look at me. "It's hard to know why people do things just by their actions. There might be more to it."

I squeezed her right hand gently but said nothing. Sometimes, it's better to listen.

"It's strange, though," she continued, her gaze still on mine. "I lived a lie, too. We both were. I thought I could tell what kind of person someone was, but I was wrong."

"No," I disagreed with a shake of my head. "You always understood me, so you're good at judging people."

"If you say so," she said, and we fell into companionable silence. I stared at my friend and now my sister-in-law and wondered why she never confided in me.

"But you should have shared your struggles with me, too. You should have, Lola," I said and meant it. The sincerity in my words cut through. "We're like inseparable twins."

Lola's smile held a touch of apology. Her eyes drifted towards Henry, who was now with the children in the garden. "I'm sorry," she whispered. "I saw how stressed you were all the time, and I didn't want to add to it. I appreciate your caring attitude and kindness."

"It's not just caring," I said to her, patting her hands. "We're here for each other, no matter what."

Lola's smile took on a mischievous glint. "Speaking of confessions and secrets, I had a crush on Henry too," she admitted. "And guess what? I only discovered he felt the same way when we met in London."

I made a face. "Oh please, spare me the details."

Lola's expression changed, and I heard the remorse in her voice when she spoke.

"I felt terrible about cheating on Daniel, and discovering that Melody wasn't his daughter broke my heart. I guess I was living a lie, too."

"Yes, you were. Everyone seems to have secrets except me!" I said with a frown. "I'm the only saint in the room."

Lola playfully threw a cushion towards me. "Come on, you're not a saint. You're in love with the village priest!"

"I'm not. He's the one pursuing me, not the other way around!" I laughed. Then paused for a moment, a wistful look on my face. "But I love this village. Sometimes I'm afraid I'll wake up and realise it was all a dream."

"Thank God, it's real," Lola said, her face creased up in a smile, aiming another cushion at me, but I grabbed it before it landed on my face.

I laughed. "Consider yourself lucky you're pregnant, or I'd have to challenge you to a wrestling match."

As a yawn escaped me, my attention shifted to the TV screen for the evening news. It was eight o'clock, and I planned to catch the news highlights before calling Shiloh and Melody back inside. It was way past their bedtime. Lola and I shared a glance, our silent understanding speaking volumes. We were both tired but felt a release from the burden of our secrets.

The news on the television played in the background, its low hum a backdrop to our contemplative silence. The room felt cocooned, a haven where confessions could be laid bare without judgment. I shifted my attention from the screen back to Lola, her face illuminated by a soft, warm light that seemed to underscore our bond.

"It's been a journey, hasn't it?" I said, breaking the silence. "Discovering truths we never thought we'd face."

Lola nodded, her eyes thoughtful. "Indeed. Life has a way of unravelling the unexpected, of leading us down paths we never imagined."

I sighed, relief and resignation washing over me at the same time. "And yet, here we are, navigating through it all, still standing."

"It's like discovering imperfection is a part of being human," she said, a faraway look in her eyes, "and embracing yourself, regardless of your shortcomings."

"Oh yeah, you're spot on," I said, glancing towards Henry playing with the children in the garden. The comforting scene served as a reminder of how our lives are no longer threatened by assassins' bullets. We're living normal, satisfying lives.

Lola's fingers played with the frayed edge of the cushion she held. "At least we're doing it together," she said.

I nodded in agreement. There was a sense of catharsis, a shared relief in opening up about the truths we had hidden for so long.

"We've got through it unscathed," I said, my voice infused with gratitude. "We've mended what's broken."

Lola looked at me, and at that moment, I saw joy radiating through her beautiful face, a spark of resilience that had always defined us. "Yes," she said, her eyes sparkling. "After all, we're stronger than the secrets we've kept."

As the evening news whispered in the background, we shared a smile and leaned back on the cushions. Our shared confessions strengthened our bond, proving that love can conquer all, including our flaws and hidden truths.

I brought out my phone to check if I had a message from Nathan, but there was nothing. I made a mental note to call him in the morning. We had planned to go for a walk and play golf, and I was already looking forward to it.

The atmosphere shifted when I noticed the horrified expression on Lola's face, and I traced her eyes to the screen. It happened just as Henry and the children re-entered the living room. All eyes were drawn to the enormous screen where Ashley's face loomed large.

My hands froze in motion, and my heartbeats were audible. I was afraid it would pop out of my chest.

Ashley is alive? How is that possible? I thought in anguish. I prayed it was a mistaken identity, like when I saw Angel's uncanny resemblance to Ashley, and I thought it was his ghost. But this looked real.

The convincing performance shattered the notion of an actor impersonating. There was no mistaking the frail and skeletal figure was Ashley. His brown hair framed his gaunt face, and as the camera zoomed in, his brown eyes shone with the same wicked glint I recognised too well. A shudder went through me when I saw that. The FBI formed a circle around him and led him into a waiting vehicle. The news team rushed to capture every moment before the car drove him away to an unknown destination.

We stared, gripped by the unfolding news. Silence engulfed the room, the unexpected news pressing down on us.

The news anchor revealed that a family visiting a loved one's grave had stumbled upon Ashley sitting naked on his grave with an eerie calmness. The silence in the room was so dense you could feel it and slice it with a knife.

The news reporter wore an uneasy expression as she handed the microphone to a man who could hardly contain his excitement and shouted, "It's a miracle!"

Lola's hand covered her mouth, her eyes wide with disbelief. Henry's expression was stern, his jaw clenched as if grappling with the incomprehensible. This was not something that fit within the bounds of the natural world. It transcended the order of things.

"When did this happen?" Lola's voice trembled as she echoed the question that hung heavy in the room.

"Just this morning," Henry replied gravely, pointing to the news ticker flashing in red beneath the screen.

An odd sensation of fear slithered up my spine, though I promptly quelled it. There was no sense in being frightened by something that defied logic. Ashley was gone, and this simply could not be him. I refused to allow the ghost of the past to haunt me.

"It's impossible. I saw him take his own life," I seethed, anger masking my disorienting emotions. I wouldn't permit myself to be trapped in the cyclone of feelings again. "I buried my husband. He must remain buried."

"What do we do?" Lola's question lingered in the air.

Henry and I exchanged a glance, our response synchronised. "We wait."

Furrowing her brows, Lola's eyes revealed potent fear. "But this changes everything. He vanished for months, and now he's returned from the dead. There's nothing normal about that. The Nephilim are going to exploit this."

With a sigh, I conceded that the theory of fallen angels might hold some validity. I ran a hand through my hair, a gesture that mirrored Ashley's.

"Death liberated me from him; besides, he wanted a divorce before he died," I murmured, my voice firm. "Whoever that was, wasn't my husband."

Lola, Henry, and I locked eyes, each of us wrestling with the gravity of the situation.

I redirected my focus when Shiloh asked, "Who's that *man*, Mum?" It served as a poignant reminder that our children were absorbing every bit of this bizarre reality.

"He's just seeking attention," Henry interrupted, taking the remote control from Shiloh and switching off the TV.

Silence blanketed us as we grappled with the repercussions of this baffling resurrection.

"Anyone want snacks?" Lola's voice punctured the silence, prompting Shiloh and Melody to scamper towards the kitchen. Henry and I withdrew to my studio and closed the door behind us.

"Try not to worry." Henry's voice enveloped me in a comforting embrace, but I recoiled from it.

"This place is my *safe* haven." I retorted, undeterred. "Whoever that man is, he won't pass through this place."

"I know," Henry said, staring at me, and I flinched. "Did you remember I promised to tell you why I blew up my Notting Hill home?"

"Yes, but you never did."

"I had to destroy some evidence, parts of my research into the fallen angels," he said, "But that day in the library when you and Shiloh came just before the attack, I found a way of destroying both the Nephilim, Ashley and his kind. I had prepared for an event like this."

I didn't like what Henry was saying.

"But if you found a way, won't that affect you, us too?" I asked, looking into his eyes.

"No, it won't. We're different. We know our birth parents, and when the time comes, trust me. Okay?"

"I trust you, Henry. You know that."

I reached for my phone in my jeans pocket, intending to call Nathan.

"Don't tell Nathan yet," Ashley said.

"Can you read my thoughts now?" I asked, incredulous at the notion.

Henry laughed, his face creasing up. "Your face and eyes betray more than you realise. You're an open book."

A soft chuckle escaped me, too. Henry had always been wise.

"Alright, big brother. Let's see how this unfolds. Perhaps it's time to start the search for Ashley's brothers. Who knows, digging into their history might expose this charlatan and end this resurrection madness," I said, opening the door for him. "I need time alone."

"Of course, but remember, we never stopped looking for his brothers. We *will* find them, even if they've stayed hidden for now. Everyone leaves traces behind," Henry said emphatically before returning to the house.

This is *my* haven, I repeated to myself. *No one will uproot me or my son from here. We stand our ground here. This is our home now, and we're done running, we're done running,* the refrain echoed in my mind.

What if the Nephilim are orchestrating this to draw us out? The thought flitted through my mind, and I dismissed it as improbable. The Sons of Nephilim's power had waned significantly since our confrontation with them in London.

I approached a painting I had completed, my eyes fixated on the angelic figure on the canvas. The celestial being stood in mid-air, robbed in white, with a gleaming golden belt around his waist. He clutched a crown of brass in his right hand and a sword in the left. His eyes shone like the sun, his tan face chiselled and set. His long hair tumbled down his back in waves. Behind him were hosts of other angels on white horses, arms raised with gleaming swords. I imagined the thunderous sounds they made as cobalt blue clouds engulfed them. The ethereal image captured my imagination, and I painted it within a day. Nathan, my confidant and friend, was enthralled by the painting, he urged me to create more. And I so did.

I knew the divine judgment upon the fallen angels was clear in Scripture, so I'm not afraid. My faith provided solace and redemption. Nothing could change that, not the ghost of a man with a questionable past, or the antics of a murderous organisation. Soon, the Nephilim will face destruction.

Then I remembered something so scary I had pushed it to the back of my mind. A sigh escaped me as I stared at my wrist. It had been itching me for over a week now. And this morning, I noticed a mark; a black star appeared—the same shape as the one on Ashley, Henry, Angel, Shiloh and now, me. Although mine was the only one, it signified the unthinkable: our link to that evil heritage. I couldn't tell Henry. *I won't tell him, yet.* I thought. He was grappling with so much right now, and this secret will stay with me.

The irony of life. Back in the house, I'd told Lola I was a saint, the only one without secrets. And here I was, hiding a mark that I knew signified an ancient curse.

Staring at the painting, I did what Nathan would encourage me to do. Kneeling before the image, I prayed—a practice I'd embraced.

Whatever the future holds, whatever battle comes my way. I would pray and fight.

There was always a battle left to fight, and I was ready.

Author's Note

As an author, I aim to create a whole new world that captures the reader's imagination. But every story has its reasons for coming to life. This second edition started small as a short tale and grew into a longer novella. Along the way, I added bits and pieces and things I've seen in the news – stories of people being mistreated and the double standards in our society.

The story I've written could happen; mysteries surround us if we take a closer look. I've explored this idea thoroughly in this edition.

Writing is often a solitary activity, and if you've read this far, I'd like to ask a favour. If you enjoyed the book and got something out of it, please leave a review online where you bought it. It might not seem like much, but it helps me as an author.

I truly hope you enjoy reading the book. There's one big, explosive battle left for Christine and her family to fight, so stay tuned.

The mentions of the *Sons of Nephilim* in the story were inspired by religious texts, like the Bible and the Book of Enoch.

Acknowledgements

A literary work takes a lot of time and preparation, be it a short story, novella or novel, but the final product differs from the first draft. I'm grateful to God Almighty for the wisdom to write this story. I am also thankful to several people for their input and contribution to this creative work.

With endless thanks to my team at Arrow Gate: Vanessa K. Williams, thanks for reading and editing. Your suggestions and input were God-sent, and I appreciate it. Dr Cam Khaski Graglia, thanks for your friendship over the years. I'm grateful for your kindness. Christy Nelson, thank you for always being there. John, I appreciate your encouragement when I wanted to stop writing and focus only on the publishing aspect. You're a lifesaver, and I appreciate you. Life is complex, and there are moments I never want to craft a story again, but John is steadfast, encouraging me not to give it up.

To my friends, thanks for reading. Roderick Low, I'm grateful for your friendship through the years. Frederick Apostoledes, thanks for reading and your kind reviews. It meant a lot to me.

To my family, my dear husband, Kay, thanks for everything, and my lovely children, Samuel, Elizabeth, and Emmanuel. Thanks for your encouragement. I appreciate it, and to my superb friends, Stella Alhassan and Sifawu

Atta, I value your friendships. Thanks for always being there.

A huge thank you to the readers and my friends worldwide, especially bloggers I've known for over a decade. I am grateful for your friendship and appreciate all that you do.

Arrow Gate is an independent publisher that plays a vital role in the success of authors. Where would we be without them? Smaller imprints release books overlooked by more prominent publishers, so thank you for your passion and dedication to the written word. The same warm thoughts go to independent bookshops worldwide that support writers and their publishers. Thank you.

S.S. David
London, 2023.

TALES OF FIVE LIES

Step into a world cloaked in darkness, where a horrifying murder hides beneath a web of lies.

Christine White lives a pampered life. She's wealthy and beautiful, but easily deceived. One cloudy night, she witnesses a crime that shatters her life. To make matters worse, the killer is still on the loose, ready to strike again. To survive, Christine must uncover the truth behind the murderer before it's too late. But what if the answers she seeks are closer to her than she ever imagined?

As the story unfolds, Christine realises her perfect life is built on lies. With time running out, she races to mend the broken pieces of her life and solve the mystery that threatens not just her, but her family, too. The ticking clock adds urgency, but the truth may turn out to be more devastating than any lie.

Explore a gripping tale of suspense, deception, and the race against time in this riveting story. Sometimes, the quest for truth comes with a price too steep to pay.

Praise for S.S. David

'A writer has the gift of being able to construct characters in three dimensions; to give them depth, personality, a back story that we as readers can empathise with. This story, although short, does that well. I found myself hooked from the very beginning, rooting for the heroine and despising the villain. What more can you ask for from a story?'
Amazon Review

'Every so often, a writer comes along who catches your eye in a new and profound way. This is that writer. She is incredible and holds a reader rapt, hanging on her every word. She strings words together in a beautifully unique way that you simply can't tear your eyes from the page.'

Frederick Apostoledes
Amazon Review